TRUSSVILLE PUBLIC LIBRARY
201 PARKWAY DRIVE
TRUSSVILLE, AL 35173
(205) 655-2022

OUTLAW VALLEY

Center Point
Large Print

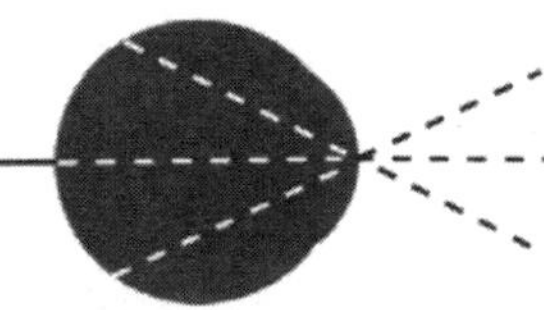

This Large Print Book carries the
Seal of Approval of N.A.V.H.

OUTLAW VALLEY

Ed La Vanway

Center Point Large Print
Thorndike, Maine

This Center Point Large Print edition is published
in the year 2016 by arrangement with
Golden West Literary Agency.

Copyright ©1960 by Ed La Vanway.
Copyright © renewed 1988 by the Estate of Ed La Vanway.

All rights reserved.

First US edition: Avalon Books.

The text of this Large Print edition is unabridged.
In other aspects, this book may vary
from the original edition.
Printed in the United States of America
on permanent paper.
Set in 16-point Times New Roman type.

ISBN: 978-1-62899-911-2 (hardcover)
ISBN: 978-1-62899-915-0 (paperback)

Publisher's Cataloging-In-Publication Data
(Prepared by The Donohue Group, Inc.)

Names: La Vanway, Ed.
Title: Outlaw valley / Ed La Vanway.
Description: Center Point Large Print edition. | Thorndike, Maine :
Center Point Large Print, 2016.
Identifiers: LCCN 2015051426 | ISBN 9781628999112 (hardcover) |
ISBN 9781628999150 (paperback)
Subjects: LCSH: Large type books. | GSAFD: Western stories.
Classification: LCC PS3562.A126 O94 2016 | DDC 813/.54—dc23

OUTLAW VALLEY

Chapter One

Migrating buffaloes travelled north and south, but along here, in getting down off the high plains, they had made a jog to the east. No buffaloes were in sight now, but their old, old trail was here. Frank Tulley had reined his big dun gelding into this trail miles back, to ride along the bank of a meandering arroyo. Other ravines, winding through cedar-dotted red-clay hills and collecting seep water, had emptied into the arroyo, until now it was a trickling stream, lined with willows. Ahead, through a haze of misting rain and the gloom of nightfall, stood the lofty trees bordering Yeguas Creek, creek of the mares.

Here and yonder to the north of Tulley huddled nester layouts, but they were all west of the Yeguas. East of the Yeguas, yonder, was G Bar L range, Garth Lenzie's range, and whatever nesters were there, like always, were six feet under. Frank Tulley hoped so, anyway.

Tulley was a G Bar L man himself, or had been until fiddling feet got him. He had quit the G Bar L to join a trail drive to the Kansas railhead, and he had stayed gone. He'd covered lots of country meanwhile. He'd been plumb out to New Mexico. At the moment he was returning from Fort Sumner, where he had helped deliver a herd of Texas longhorns to an Indian-beef contractor.

Reed Anthony was the drover.

Trailing out, Anthony had pointed his herd to the south-west along the Southern Overland Mail trace to the Horsehead Crossing of the Pecos and then up the river. With the cattle disposed of at Bosque Redondo, Anthony had paid Tulley off, and Tulley had succumbed to his old weakness.

In fancy he had seen and smelled and touched Katie Lenzie, and that had brought him back to his old stomping grounds as fast as he could travel, following a water-hole map sketched for him by a Mexican *comanchero.*

Three hours from now, he told himself exultantly, he would be at the G Bar L headquarters.

Even so, damn it, his craving wouldn't be completely satisfied, not tonight. Katie would be in bed, asleep, and nobody's girl, after a separation of five years, was going to jump up and welcome him with a hug and a kiss.

Five years had been a long time to Katie, as young as she was.

Tulley now recalled Garth Lenzie's parting words: "Are you feeling sorry for them sodbusters?"

"No," Tulley had said truthfully.

"You don't mind fighting to make my deadline stick? You'll shoot to kill for it?"

"Who do you want shot?"

"Nobody! What in hell's the matter with you? Wanting more money?"

"Garth, I'll tell you—I just can't stand it around here with Katie gone."

The old rawhider had laughed fit to bust. "Pshaw! That gal is trying to get you bored for the simples, Frank!"

Tulley had professed love for Katie.

Sobering, the girl's father had said, "Well, she don't love you, not the way you want her to. Sometimes I doubt she's got that kind of love in her. Don't borrow trouble, Frank. Don't set your heart on any woman. It ain't done that way. Your woman will lasso you."

Katie had gone East to stay with Garth's sister while she got finished up at some sort of female-breaking corral, and Frank Tulley reckoned that was the proper thing for her. She was a top hand at everything except book learning. Chances were she would pick that up right fast, too.

Katie had been seventeen then, and the only schooling she'd had she'd gotten from a widow that Garth had brought in from Weatherford. Now she was twenty-two. And educated, by God. That might make a difference.

Those five years had been long ones to Frank Tulley, too, and mostly because he hadn't heard a word from the G Bar L in all that time.

Yeah, everything might be different here now. Garth had been an old man then. He would be as grey-headed as a rat now. Maybe he had passed on to his reward. Why, anything could have happened. Somebody else might own the G Bar L. Katie could have taken a husband while back East. Those fellows back there were slick talkers, and Katie hadn't had any experience with men like that. Let one of them find out she stood to inherit a big cattle spread, and they would grab her. Pronto.

Now that he was nearly there, Frank Tulley found himself checking the stride of his dun, not increasing it. He wanted to know about the G Bar L, but he dreaded finding out.

Obscured by nightfall and low-scudding clouds, Yeguas Valley spread out before him in a pattern of wooded creeks, timbered hills, mesquite benches and short-grass flats. The G Bar L headquarters lay almost due east. To the northeast, down Yeguas Creek, was Buffalo City, which Garth Lenzie himself had laid out.

Garth had had the town site surveyed and platted and had helped get the settlement started when the nesters first came into the valley, but he hadn't counted on the hoemen flocking in, in droves, trying to grab every foot of land Garth owned.

Unwilling to lose all of Yeguas Creek, Garth had ordered the grangers to halt at Double Mountain, and he'd been fiercely determined to make that deadline stick. Frank Tulley hoped that it had.

Nesters were all right, a certain amount of them. Cornbread and turnip greens was all right, too, with a glass of buttermilk and a couple of green onions, but a man wasn't going to work no twelve-hour day on it. You had to have meat, like this venison here on the saddle. But you couldn't raise deer meat enough for everybody, so you raised longhorns. Now you're not going to keep longhorns penned up like chickens. They had to have range. And somebody had to fight the nesters off of it. Yes, Tulley reckoned that's what he had come back to do, if sodbusters were still giving the G Bar L trouble . . .

Riding on down into the bottom, Tulley found a sheltered spot and dismounted. Little chance he would have of talking the G Bar L cook out of a meal by the time he reached the ranch, so he would eat now.

From his pommel strings he took a tallowed sack which contained the hunk of venison, and he got a blackened tomato tin and a poke of parched coffee beans from his saddlebags and put them on a flat rock. The gelding became restive as Tulley did this.

Whinnying, tossing its head, the horse acted as though it heard, or saw, or smelled another bronc; one of the wild mares this valley was noted for, perhaps. Tulley stood still and listened. He heard only the wind through the trees, spattering raindrops.

Years back, Tulley would have been scared of a redskin. This valley had long been Kiowa and Comanche country, but they no longer pitched their lodges in it, because the bluebellies and the galvanized Yankees had driven them into Indian Territory. They'd done it to keep the Texas Rangers from being reorganized.

A man couldn't bet a freshly curried scalp on that, however. Pulling his Henry rifle from the saddle boot, Tulley jacked a cartridge into the firing chamber and peered about in the darkness.

He heard something running.

A horse. Tulley heard it crash through a patch of brush. It continued, toward the north-east, its receding hoofbeats smothered by the wind. Tulley put the rifle away.

He set about gathering wood and building a fire, and after he had a blaze going, he took care of the gelding, loosening the cinches and pulling off the bridle. He used his lariat to stake the horse out on a nearby grassy knoll. The gelding was quiet now, so Tulley went back and got water from the creek and put it on to boil. He used the surface of the rock and the butt of his Remington six-gun to pulverize some coffee beans. Afterwards he sliced and salted strips of the deer meat to broil on willow spits stuck in the sand around his fire.

The blended smells of sizzling venison fat and bubbling coffee had honed his hunger to an edge when again he heard a commotion downstream. This time the sounds were less alarming. It was the noise of men and horses. They were speculating on Tulley's occupation, and came toward him, jogging single file among the trees and into the periphery of the firelight.

A familiar voice said, "It's Frank, all right. Probably just hit the valley, and he's been gone four or five years."

All three were belted with six-guns and rode with rifles across their saddlebows. The one in the lead was a lanky, lantern-jawed redhead whom Tulley had never seen before. Tulley didn't know the second man, either—a dark-looking, spade-bearded fellow. The one who'd identified Tulley was a bronc stomper Garth Lenzie had sometimes hired to shape up the remuda. He was scrawny, middle-aged Lige Wessels.

"How are you, Lige? Howdy, men. Light down and pitch in."

None of the three dismounted.

Lige Wessels said, "I'm just tolerable, Frank. Have you come back to stay?" There was a furtiveness about him, an arrogance about the other two.

"I don't know, Lige. Hope so. I will if I can hire out to the G Bar L again. Does Lenzie still run it?"

Wessels said, "Yeah, he's still there. He's just hanging on by the skin of his teeth, though. And he ain't got no teeth!"

"Lige," the redhead said sharply, "you talk too much."

Frank Tulley stiffened. "Say, Red, do you own the English language? If you do, we'll *habla* in *Español*. We was saddlemates."

The redhead bristled. He braced his boots in the stirrups and said, "If you want Lige's tail caught in a crack, you just keep orating, there, Mr. Tulley. He knows too much already."

Lige said, "Ah, Griff, keep your shirt on. Where have you been gone to, Frank?"

"New Mexico. Working for a man named Reed Anthony. He took a herd of steers to some carpet-baggers over at Fort Sumner. Quite a man. I thought I knowed it all till I met up with him."

Wessels said, "I've heard of him."

The spade-bearded man had looked Tulley over closely, from high-heeled boots and Levi's to blue bandanna and big white hat.

"Anyone come down this way recent?" he asked. "We're tracking a horse thief."

"Any horse thief tracks around my fire here, you're welcome to inspect them."

The lantern-jawed redhead said, "Shut up, Jules. What do you think, Lige?"

"I say don't pay any mind to Frank Tulley. He always tends to his own business, without you ask him to tend to yours."

There was a moment of silence with the wind rushing through the wet leaves and swirling in eddies to whip smoke into Tulley's eyes and to fan the fire brighter. The venison was done. Tulley began moving the spits back from the fire.

"Sure smells good," Wessels said.

"I asked you to light down and pitch in, didn't I?"

Wessels glanced questioningly at Griff, but the redhead said, "Hell, no. If you're hungry, just tighten that belt another notch. We've got to catch that horse thief." Lifting the reins and jerking his head, he snapped, "Come on."

They rode back the way they had come.

The sound of their departure soon halted, as if they had changed their minds. Tulley heard them arguing. The man called Jules said, "These tracks was made just a little bit ago. That Tulley was lying."

Griff said, "He was more than that. He was looking me and you over like he would rather side a horse thief any time as us."

Lige Wessels said, "Don't mess with him. Just don't you mess with him."

They rode on.

The thunderstorm was getting closer, with flashes of lightning illuminating the thrashing treetops and flickering in the gloomy aisles of the creek-bottom woods. Tulley ate the venison and drank the coffee. After smoking a cigarette he brought in his horse, then kicked sand over the sputtering embers of his fire before he climbed into the saddle.

A rain-laden breeze smote him on the back of the head and put a damp smell of wood smoke into his nostrils as he walked his horse in the direction taken by the three men. He picked up their trail when the lightning flashed.

It was none of his put-in, Tulley realized, but Wessels was wrong. He had been speaking of the Frank Tulley who existed five years ago. *This* Frank Tulley had a mite more sense. He knew now that the more a man minded his own business, the less and less business he came to have. And he saw he couldn't just head straight for the G Bar L and ignore the possibility that a fellow human being might become host of a necktie party in the dark of these woods.

Riding on, Tulley lost the trail of Lige, Griff and Jules because of continued darkness, and after a while he broke out into a natural clearing. He was getting wet now, and stopped to put on his slicker. Suddenly, on the far side of the meadow, a hoarse shout of surprise lifted. A rapid thud of hoofbeats came toward Tulley. Gunfire rang out, muzzle flame of carbines distinctly visible.

Tulley made a quick decision. Not yet having untied the slicker, he sprang back astride the gelding and put it into a run. He pursued the stampeding bronc by sound. It stepped on its bridle rein and stumbled. By the time it was up and whirling, Tulley's gelding was alongside it. Tulley grabbed the bronc's bit ring. It bore no rider, no saddle, even. But no need for those fellows to know it. With a quick movement, Tulley jerked the bronc's headstall off, and the mustang sprang forward. It stampeded into the rainy darkness again, the pound of its hoofs bringing fresh yells and more gunshot from the pursuers.

Tulley steadied his gelding and remained motionless. In the direction they were headed, Lige and Jules and Griff would pass Tulley unnoticed unless lightning illuminated him.

The sky remained dark. Jules and Lige and Griff rode beyond hearing.

Tossing the bridle into the grass, Tulley rode on across the meadow. At the edge of the woods he stopped to listen. He heard only the sounds of the storm. He cupped hands to his mouth.

"Hey, fellow, let's make tracks. I've got a horse here that'll carry double."

No answer came.

Maybe those slugs had knocked him off that bronc. Tulley began riding in circles, combing the area where the gun flashes had seemed to be. No luck. Maybe the fellow had hit the ground running, and if he was one of those long-legged nesters, he was two miles away by now. All at once then, the gelding shied.

"Easy, boy," Tulley said, and, in a louder tone, "Don't shoot! If you stole a horse, likely you had to do it. I read the earmarks on those skunks, especially that Griff somebody."

Still no answer.

Yet someone was there on the ground in front of the gelding. No mistake about it. This horse could almost talk.

Suddenly Tulley caught a sound that cut him to the quick. It was a suppressed sob. He dismounted. He moved around in front of his horse and ground-hitched it. Digging a lucifer out of his Levi's, Tulley scratched it alight and cupped his hands against the wind. He hunkered down. The person was clad in denims, hickory shirt and slouch hat. Tulley saw clenched teeth, tear-wet cheeks. His face flushed. The "horse thief" was a yellow-haired girl. Woman, maybe, judging from that shirt front.

"Are you hurt?"

"My shoulder," she whimpered.

The match went out, but Tulley had seen no blood on the girl's rain-dampened clothing.

"What's wrong with your shoulder?"

"My horse bolted."

Tulley stood erect, eyes turned upward. He reached up and felt the limb that had swept the girl from her horse as the bronc ran under it.

"I'll help you up," Tulley said. He started to lift her, but she cried out with pain.

The thunderstorm was moving on. The sky overhead was a solid mass of cloud now, and a steady drizzle had set in. Leaning forward to shield the flame with hat and body, Tulley lit another lucifer. He saw by the expression on the girl's face that she was suffering badly. He reached for his bowie and in the darkness began carefully to cut away a fistful of her shirt.

She flinched, crying out again.

"I know it hurts, ma'am, but I've got to do it. Your shoulder's dislocated. How does it feel—fingers tingle and seem numb?"

"Yes."

"That's what it is. You'd better get set for some misery. I'll have to hurt you pretty bad."

He moved her so that he could take her by the shoulders from behind, then placed a knee in her back and gave a sudden wrench. She didn't yell, and he knew she had fainted. He waited a moment, undecided; then he bundled her in his slicker and picked her up. He waded back across the meadow with her, leading his horse.

The embers of his cooking fire were still glowing when he pushed aside the sand, and he secured dry fuel from a pile of driftwood. When he had a bright blaze going, he inspected the girl's shoulder. It didn't seem to be badly bruised. There was nothing more Tulley could do for her, except stay with her. He sat down beside her on the spread slicker.

Finally he said, "You're playing possum."

She jerked her eyes open and sat up fearfully.

"I won't bother you," he said.

She sat there with downcast eyes. The hurt in

her was more than an injured shoulder, he suspected, and he asked, "Ever hear of Frank Tulley?"

"No."

"Your people are sodbusters. Didn't you ever hear them cussing me?"

She moved her head sideways.

"You-all haven't been here long. I used to be pretty well hated in this valley, but I've been gone a spell. The nester population has probably had a turnover since I was here."

She kept her gaze on the fire and said nothing. Her hair was as yellow as gold, and her features, even in this unhappy moment, were lovely.

"What's your name?"

"Marie Simpson."

"Why were those men trying to gun you off of that bronc? I know Lige Wessels, and he wouldn't take a second look at a broomtail like you were riding."

She wouldn't say anything.

"What's Griff's last name? And Jules's?"

"I don't know."

"Now you're lying to me. Is that the way to do when I'm trying to help you?"

In tear-choked tones of indignation, she said, "Well, how can I tell you about something I don't understand myself? I'm not sure. I don't know. Why did he—" She broke off and fell silent.

"Are you married?"

She frowned through her tears. “No.”

“You’ve got a home, though.”

“But I’m afraid to go there. My father might get mixed up in it.”

Tulley got up and busied himself chunking up the fire. “If you can figure out some place for me to take you, I’ll be glad to do it.”

“Let me go with you.”

“I haven’t got any place to go.”

“You were going somewhere.”

“Well, I’ll tell you, Marie; I’m headed for the G Bar L ranch headquarters. You know Katie Lenzie. At least you’ve seen her. And if she’s at the ranch, I sure wouldn’t want to ride in there in the middle of the night with you. She’s a fine girl, but she wouldn’t stand for anything like that.”

“Well, go on, then, and leave me right here.”

Tulley hunkered on his spurs, watching raindrops sputter in the ashes of the fire.

Marie said, “I didn’t ask you to butt in, but you did. Now you can just butt right out again.”

Tulley ignored her. He said reflectively, “If Tom Bradshaw is still the cook there, he can fix you up. Tom used to be a full-fledged doctor. Yes, I reckon I’d better take you there, Katie or no Katie.”

He had to make room for her, though, and he cached his tarp-covered bedroll, war sack and saddlebags at the foot of a cottonwood. He lifted Marie up behind the cantle and folded the slicker around her, then went over to put the fire out, but suddenly stopped to listen. He left the fire burning and got into the saddle.

"If you get sick, Marie, let me know."

"I'm sick now."

"I mean sick enough to fall off. Hold tight to me." He reined toward the creek.

"This isn't the way."

"I heard voices. I think those fellows are coming back."

Choosing a spot in the thicket where he could clearly see the area around the campfire, Tulley dismounted and got his rifle. He waited there, ready to pinch the gelding's nose to prevent discovery, and in less than five minutes Griff and Jules and Lige again rode up to the fire. They didn't have the girl's horse.

The lantern-jawed Griff dismounted. He pushed Tulley's bedroll clear of the tree and unrolled it. He dumped the contents of Tulley's saddlebags on to the sand—razor and strop and brush, all the odds and ends needed by a man on the trail—and kicked it into the blaze. The redhead heaved Tulley's soogans and tarp on to the fire, too, and Tulley couldn't restrain himself any longer.

Shouldering through the brush, he shouted, "Don't burn my bedding!"

The redhead whirled with drawn gun and shot, and ran for his horse. The bullet slammed against

Tulley's leg and knocked him down. He got up. More gunshots roared and flashed at him, and he felt his hat go. Favouring his left leg, he reared back to a sitting position and tried to point the Henry rifle at the rearing and plunging horses there at the fire. He started shooting. Gunsmoke obscured his vision, and he heard the sound of departing hoofbeats. Tulley cursed vigorously.

They were coyotes. They'd had him at their mercy and hadn't had guts enough to finish the job. Another thought quickly intruded, however. Maybe Lige Wessels had saved him, had told it scary and high-tailed it, filling the other two with panic.

With the acrid smell of exploded powder and burning wool coiling among the trees, Tulley pushed to his feet and limped back to his horse and Marie.

"Good," he grunted. "I was afraid a ricochet might have gotten you."

In a high, thin voice, she asked, "How are you? You're not badly wounded, are you?"

"Nicked in the leg. Nothing to be alarmed about. We'll make it to the G Bar L, maybe."

Chapter Two

By midnight the thunderstorm had passed on; a summer breeze was fast drying up the countryside, and overhead the sky was ablaze with stars. Having gotten lost, Tulley had struck the Buffalo City road away to the north-west of the ranch, and had had to backtrack for a distance. This road passed the corrals and stables. Tulley kept going straight ahead to the tree-shaded eminence on which the ranch house sat.

The Lenzie home was a sprawling frame structure that would have done credit to any town. Here in western Texas it was a mansion. Garth had hired freighters to haul shingles, doors, window sash and other materials all the way from San Antonio. The windows of the house were lamp-lighted now, which was unusual at this time of night. It could be, then, Tulley told himself, that Wessels and the other two had been here recently. Maybe they were still here.

Tulley had Marie in front of him now, cradled against the saddlebow and his chest. He had lost the slicker. Once he had become dizzy from his leg wound and had tumbled off his horse with the girl. He had cursed in clumsy frustration when trying to get back into the saddle. He'd made it, of course, but it had been an ordeal. Marie hadn't uttered a sound.

Afterward she had become feverish, crying out, "Why did he unload it?" and she had mumbled incoherently. She had flung herself out of his arms once. On guard now, he held her tight.

A pack of hounds rushed down from the house, bawling, loping down the slope in strung-out fashion, the younger dogs in front. All were too experienced with mustangs, however, to approach too close to the gelding's teeth and hoofs.

When Tulley reached the hitching rail near the front gallery, he called out loudly for Garth Lenzie.

No reply came from inside the house.

Unmindful of the dogs, Tulley tossed the reins over the rail and slid to the ground, Marie Simpson in his arms.

A man wearing noisy spurs had followed Tulley up from the bunkhouses. Coming on into the lamplight, he said, "What do you want? What's the matter with that woman? Who is she—with britches on?" There was a sneer in his tone.

Tulley waited until the man had scolded the dogs into silence, and then he said, "Where's Garth? Effie? Katie?"

"They're in town. What do you want?"

"This girl's horse stampeded. She got kicked off by a limb. I want to put her to bed. She needs care. Is Tom Bradshaw still the cook here?"

"Uh-huh."

"Go get him. Tell him Frank Tulley is here with a nester girl he found out on the range, hurt."

The man said, "I hope you're not mixing us up in somebody else's damned troubles," and then went down the slope toward the lighted cook-shack.

Tulley stood there with Marie in his arms, his leg paining him, impatience gnawing him. He saw the pair coming up the slope within a reasonable length of time, but they didn't approach the front gallery. They took the path to the rear one. Boots and spurs sounded inside the house presently, and the two came through it on to the front porch.

Bradshaw was short of stature, wore his sandy hair clipped and had added quite a bit to his paunch since Tulley had seen him last. The moustache which studded his upper lip looked as neat as ever, though.

He stared a moment. "Are you bringing her, Frank, or is someone sending her?"

"I don't understand you, Tom, but her being here is my idea."

"Bring her on in."

Tulley grunted, ascending the steps.

"She just hit a limb. She hasn't been shot, eh?" Bradshaw asked.

"She was shot *at,* Tom."

The other man said dourly, "Hope we don't get blamed for that."

The ex-doctor leaned forward for a closer look

at the girl in the lamplight of the gallery. "That's Mose Simpson's daughter. When she comes to, she'll probably have hysterics at being on the G Bar L."

"She knew she was coming here. She said she didn't have any place else to go. Let's put her to bed."

Bradshaw went back into the hallway, Tulley following him with Marie. Tentatively the *cocinero* peered into rooms on either side of the hall. "Here's one we can put her in," he said. He went and lit a lamp. Noticing Tulley's limp, he asked, "Is that your own blood on your britches, Frank?"

"I expect," Tulley said. He carried Marie into the room and toward the bed. It was a guest room, decorated for a woman.

"Lay her down, Frank—wait a minute. I'll slip her shoes off."

Marie's face was flushed. She jerked her eyes open, a wild look in them. "Tulley!" she cried.

"I'm here. I've still got you. We're at the G Bar L now, Marie, and this man right here is a doctor. Don't you worry about a thing."

"Don't leave me."

"I won't leave you."

When they had got her on the bed, Bradshaw said, "I'll go get some water."

The other man was lounging in the hall doorway. He was a sharp-faced fellow of medium build, squint-eyed, and though he was barely thirty-five years old, he had a shaggy head of grey hair. He stepped aside for Bradshaw to leave the room. Pointing a finger at Tulley's leg, he said, "That's a bullet hole, and it got meat. Who shot you?"

"I don't know."

"Did Marie do it?"

"Do you think she'd be shooting me one minute and hugging my neck the next?"

"I know—Jess Burk shot you! Why, you're the one who killed—"

"I'm going to knock your teeth down your throat if you don't shut up."

Jerking his shaggy head back in startled fashion, the man ducked out of the room.

The *cocinero* returned, bringing a pitcher of water and a glass, a bottle of black medicine and a spoon. He smelled of soap. His arms were damp.

"Raise her up, Frank."

Tulley lifted Marie so that Bradshaw could get some of the medicine down her. Afterward, Bradshaw let her quench her thirst, and he said to Tulley, "You look as if you're choking for a drink, yourself."

"I'll go to the pump."

"Well, you ought to remember your way around."

"It's been changed some. Fancied up."

"Katie's idea." Bradshaw put the pitcher and glass on a nearby table where he'd set the medicine. “Gil will be here with my saddlebags in just a minute, Frank,” he said, and almost immediately the sharp-faced man came back into the bedroom. “Put them on that chair, Gil. Frank Tulley is one of the old-timers here, Gil. He left about five years ago. Frank, Gil Jebb is the *segundo*.”

Tulley said, “He talks like he’s the owner.”

“By God, I’ll come closer to owning it than you ever will.”

After an amused silence, Bradshaw said, “Frank, he probably will, at that, the way things are turning out.”

“What do you mean?”

“Garth’s losing his tail hold.”

“Well,” Tulley said, “we’ll just slow the critter down and let him get both hands on it.”

The foreman handed Bradshaw a pair of spectacles. “Need my help with her, Tom?”

“No, I don’t, Gil, but I’d take it as a favour if you’d have somebody take care of Tulley’s horse.”

“No,” Tulley said. “I’ll do that myself.”

“You stay here,” Bradshaw ordered. “When I finish with Marie, I’m going to take care of that bullet hole of yours.”

Giving Tulley a bright cut from hostile eyes, the shaggy-haired foreman left the room.

Putting his glasses on, Bradshaw took a pair of scissors from a saddlebag and snipped away more of Marie’s clothing. “Bring that lamp,

Frank. Hold it close here." With Tulley holding the light, Bradshaw examined Marie's shoulder.

"Still out of joint?"

"No. It's all right." Bradshaw straightened up. "I'm through with the light. Put it on the dresser yonder and then step out into the hall until I call you."

Tulley limped out to the pump on the rear gallery for a drink, and to scrub his hands and face and head. He came back to wait in the hall, and had time to smoke two cigarettes before Bradshaw summoned him back into Marie's bedroom.

"I put a compress under her arm and bound it to her side. If it looks all right in a day or so, I'll let her carry her arm in a sling. It isn't bad; she's really suffering from exhaustion. And grief. She lost her intended husband today. Or yesterday, rather; it's after midnight." Bradshaw didn't give Tulley time to speak. He pointed. "That's Katie's room over there, Frank. Go get me one of her nightgowns."

Tulley said, "Marie was talking about someone unloading a gun. What did she mean? How did her intended husband die?"

Bradshaw shook his head. "I don't know what she meant. The man she planned to marry got shot or stabbed or burned up—I don't know the details. Garth and Vince are in jail for it. Vince Potter, one of the hands."

Tulley stared, uncomprehending.

"A county has been organized since you left, Frank. The sheriff came and got them. Sheriff Al Ramage. He brought a posse with him."

"Was that fellow a nester?"

"Yes. Jess Burk. He was killed and his place burned. He'd taken up some land this side of Double Mountain, so that made Garth circumstantially guilty. Garth has always been so walleyed touchy about any sodbuster coming past his deadline there."

Tulley met Bradshaw's gaze, holding it. "Did Garth and Vince Potter do it?"

"Well, I don't know. I don't really give a damn. But Garth said they didn't, and I believe him. Garth admitted having cuss fights with Burk and threatening to do it. He'd been quarrelling with Burk for six months, every time he passed there. So yesterday morning somebody did it for Garth —killed Burk and burned his house and barn."

"Any idea why?"

"Sure. I have it all figured out to suit my own opinion." Bradshaw glanced at the girl on the bed, sleeping under the influence of the medicine. "Go get that gown, Frank."

"That's why you said she would have hysterics being here?"

Bradshaw nodded.

Tulley crossed the hall and lit one of Katie's lamps. He searched through her fragrant clothespress and he took Bradshaw a silk nightgown trimmed with blue ribbons.

Tulley wasn't really thinking of Marie, or of Katie, either, now. He was concerned with the plight of the G Bar L owner, and he said, "There ought to be some way we can get Garth out of that hoosegow."

Bradshaw countered, "Raise her up, so I can get this on her." They got the gown on Marie without uncovering her or arousing her.

"It's all in knowing how, Tom."

"I've delivered young ones that way, Frank, with a sheet over them, among a roomful of people." Tom Bradshaw sighed. "But I've told you the sad story of my misspent life at least twice."

"I thought you'd be back practising medicine by now, though."

"I keep telling myself I'll do it next year. Or next month. Or next week. But I never quite reach the I'll-do-it-now stage."

"Well, I intend to see that you do. I'll load your stuff up and haul it to Buffalo City, and make you do it, Tom."

Someone entered the hallway from the rear gallery, and the foreman came in, carrying Tulley's saddle gun. "I could have put this in the bunkhouse, but I didn't want to go without burying the hatchet with Tulley, if he aims to take a riding job here."

Tulley took the gun. "I won't join the outfit as long as you're foreman."

Gil Jebb looked at Bradshaw. "Empty shell in his gun. Magazine about half-full. Maybe we ought to ask him about Jess Burk, with Jess killed and him showing up here with Jess's girl. And her unconscious."

Bradshaw kept a straight face. "It does look kind of suspicious, Gil."

"Hell, yes. Tulley's been gone a spell. Gone where? He never come in off no long trail. He's got a fresh haircut, and he didn't have no hat. There wasn't anything on his saddle, either."

"A Mexican sheepherder up on the *llano* cut my hair, Gil. My hat and the rest of my stuff is up on the south-west range, what wasn't burned up by Lige Wessels and a couple of fellows called Griff and Jules. The empty shell in my gun is the last one I fired at them when they gave me this game leg."

Jebb nodded.

"You won't ever make me sore by defending Garth Lenzie, Gil," Frank added.

The foreman relaxed. "That was Griff Spaugh and Jules Carnotte. I can understand now. It's pretty easy to have a run-in with them. That Spaugh is too low-down even to stomp."

As the foreman started out, Bradshaw said, "Send me someone to sit up with this girl, Gil."

"Who do you want?"

"Obie Sheppard is all right around ladies."

"I'll roust him out," Jebb said. He left the house.

Bradshaw had attended to Tulley's leg before Sheppard arrived. Sheppard was twenty-five, slim of build, with grey eyes and a shock of curly blond hair. He was belted with a six-gun and carried a carbine.

"Come in here, Obie," Bradshaw said. "Frank, Obie Sheppard is the best hand in the outfit, to my thinking. Effie says so, too."

Sheppard held out his hand, and Tulley shook with him. "I've heard a lot about you," the youth said. "I came here the week after you left. The outfit sort of fell apart when you took off."

"It wasn't on account of me, Obie. It fell apart because Katie went East."

"Well, that might have had something to do with it." Sheppard put his attention on the girl. "Is Marie going to be all right, Tom?"

Bradshaw nodded.

Sheppard said, "Gil told me that Carnotte and Spaugh and Wessels were gunning for Tulley. Reckon they might show up here?"

"They might," Tom Bradshaw said. "I'd blow the lamp out in here, Obie, and those in the hall. I'd put my chair there in the hall, and that way you can keep an eye on both doors."

Tulley looked from one to the other. "If they come here, they'll do it openly. Lige Wessels wouldn't be a party to sneaking around the G Bar L."

"You've got more confidence in him than I have," Bradshaw said.

"I know him better. Lige would back-shoot anybody for a plugged peso, but he's got too much respect for this outfit to try to prowl."

"The dogs all know him," Bradshaw said. "He could get away with it."

"Well, there's not any use of you fellows worrying," Obie said, patting his carbine.

"No," Bradshaw said. "Let's go, Frank."

They went past bedrooms, the dining room and the kitchen to the rear gallery. The cookshack, with the front part of the building lamplighted, stood to the north. Two smaller structures, the smokehouse and storeroom, lay behind it. Farther north were the two bunkhouses, one for the G Bar L riders and another for the *braceros* who came and went, according to season work on the ranch. The blacksmith shed, corrals and stables, wagon shed and barns were scattered out down the long slant of undulating slope to the north. The horizon to the east was shortened by a high, steep ridge.

When they reached the cookshack, Bradshaw said, "Go on in, Frank. Help yourself, if you're hungry. I'll be right back." He walked on toward the other buildings.

Tulley entered the lamplighted part of the

cookshack and scouted around for something to tempt his appetite. Not being hungry, he passed up the beans that Bradshaw was cooking for breakfast, and got a coffee cup from those stacked in the centre of one of the tables where the hands ate.

Bradshaw's living quarters were in the rear half of this building, and Tulley recalled the time the ex-doctor had fallen in love with a Buffalo City widow. Figuring on getting hitched, Tom had hauled in a wagonload of new furniture to spruce up his rooms. The marriage had never come off, for some reason unknown to Tulley, but doubtless Tom still had the furniture back there.

Bradshaw entered the cookshack and tossed a couple of sacks of makings on to the table where Tulley sat drinking coffee. "Know where you lost your hat, Frank?"

"Up on the north-west range."

"I thought we had hats, but we've run out. You can borrow my Sunday-go-to-meeting hat till you get to town. If you're short, buy whatever you need at John Pemberton's store and charge it to the brand."

"I've got money, Tom. This money belt you were eyeing isn't stuffed with washers."

Bradshaw went to the stove and brought the coffeepot. "Let me fill your cup. I'm going to take Obie Sheppard some of this."

"Obie's got a crooked eye, Tom."

"No. He's a good man, Frank. Do to ride the river with."

"That wasn't what I meant, Tom. He's a born killer. He may go all the way through life without it ever coming to the surface. But I know a killer eye when I see one."

"Maybe so," Bradshaw agreed. He took a cup and the three-gallon coffeepot and went out.

He was back soon.

"Marie awake?" Tulley asked.

"No. I gave her some laudanum." Bradshaw sat down across the table from Tulley. "What made her horse stampede?"

"Lige and those fellows were shooting at her, Tom."

"Risking their necks. I wonder why."

"She wouldn't tell me. What do Carnotte and Spaugh do for a living—help Lige catch mustangs?"

Bradshaw shook his head. "They fetch and carry for Webb Colter."

"Who's he?"

"He came to Buffalo City shortly after you left, Frank. Came originally from St. Louis. They say he's the black sheep of a well-to-do family. Kin to the Chouteaus. Sort of a curious duck. He owns the fanciest saloon in town, but spends more time with the sodbusters. He's settled a lot of them west of the Yeguas, and he's put a few of them on G Bar L range."

Tulley emptied the cup and pushed it aside. "Below Double Mountain?"

"Of course."

"If anyone makes money out of that land down there, Tom, it ought to be Garth. He gave it up voluntarily. He could have kept those sodbusters out to begin with if he'd wanted to. If that fellow Colter is making money by locating nesters, I'd make him pay. You say this is a county now—Garth could take him to court. If Garth wasn't in jail himself, that is."

Bradshaw rubbed his moustache. "Garth doesn't own that land, Frank. He never did."

"What are you saying? Garth told me he bought this valley fair and square when he moved out here from Kentucky."

Bradshaw nodded. "That's what *he* thought. But what he actually bought, Frank, was a quitclaim deed to the old Contreras grant, a Spanish land grant. But the Contreras family never did receive a grant from the Mexican government after the revolution, so the Republic of Texas wouldn't confirm the title. And naturally, the state of Texas never did, either. Webb Colter proved that to Garth with a lawyer."

Tulley frowned but said nothing.

"I think Webb Colter is behind Garth's being in jail," Tom Bradshaw went on. "My idea is that Colter killed Jess Burk or had him killed, to frame Garth. When Garth found out he didn't really own this ranch, he hustled around and bought some land scrip. He got enough to locate a section at each of our water holes. It just about broke him, though, with the cost of surveying."

Tulley made a gesture of impatience. "That's all he really needs. With the water holes cinched, he can hold all this upper range."

"You talk in terms of running cattle, Frank. Those nesters will try to farm anything. They'll dig-wells and use a rope and bucket."

"Colter wants to bring them past Double Mountain, you think?" Tulley asked.

"I figure that way. And Jess Burk's being wiped out will make those hoemen mad as hornets. They'll be more determined than ever to grab this upper range. Furthermore, Colter's given them land scrip at a dollar an acre."

Tulley gave his chin a jerk. "I've seen those certificates pass for five cents an acre in poker games, right there in Buffalo City."

"And nobody wanted them. Too bad Garth couldn't have known what was ahead of him. Webb Colter banked on that scrip. They say that he has a whole trunkful of it." The *cocinero* pointed. "Want some more coffee, Frank?"

"No. Wasn't Garth and Vince Potter here at the ranch when Burk was killed?"

"Yeah. But they'd just come back from town. If Colter was set on framing Garth, he'd wait until he was positive Garth was vulnerable." Bradshaw yawned. “Between you and me, Frank, Gil Jebb isn’t going to lift a hand to peel that hoosegow off of Garth. Why don’t you do it? Take the boys over to Buffalo City and tree that town.”

“We’ll see.” Tulley pushed back his chair. “Where’ll I sleep?”

“Same old bunk.”

“I ought to be able to find that,” Tulley said. He picked up his carbine and limped out of the cookshack.

Chapter Three

Entering the darkened bunkhouse as quietly as possible, Frank Tulley placed the carbine on the pegs over the bunk where he had placed a similar gun many times before. Taking off only his gun-belt and boots, he stretched out on the bed and went to sleep.

The bunkhouse was still dark when he awakened, but it was nearly daybreak. Coyotes were yapping loudly on the ridge to the east, and that was a familiar sound, almost a clock, to Tulley. They always grew noisier as daylight approached. Suddenly, at the sound of boot steps outside, Tulley swung off the bunk. In view of the trouble here yesterday and last night, he wanted to know who was stirring at this early hour. Carrying his boots, he left the bunkhouse.

He met Bradshaw. "Anything wrong, Tom?"

"The girl. She's awake, and seems scared to death, Frank. Thinks you have ridden on, and won't take my word for it. Will you come and show her you're still here?"

"Sure," Tulley said. He began pulling on his boots. "Did she tell you anything more about Wessels and those fellows?"

"Not yet."

The two of them walked up the slope to the

ranch house and went in the front way. They found Obie Sheppard in an easy chair brought into the hall from the parlour. He looked sleepy, which meant he'd really kept a vigil.

Tulley grinned. "You'll do to ride the river with, Obie. Make it all right?"

"Didn't see hide nor hair of those fellows, Frank."

"They probably headed for Buffalo City."

A lamp was burning in Marie's bedroom. Walking in ahead of Bradshaw, Tulley approached her bed, asking, "How are you feeling?"

A happy glow entered her eyes as she watched him. "I'm all right," she said.

Bradshaw said, "She hasn't got a bit of fever." He moved up on the opposite side of the bed. "Now that Frank's here, Marie, why don't you tell about that business last night? Why were Lige Wessels and Carnotte and Spaugh trying to kill you?"

"They weren't trying to kill me. They wanted Jess Burk's horse that I was riding, because he owed them for it."

Bradshaw shook his head. "He didn't owe them for it, Marie. Lige Wessels won't sell his mustangs that way. Takes cash money to get a horse from him."

"Jess told me he owed them."

Silent a moment, Bradshaw said, "We'll let your folks know where you are."

"But I don't want to go home!"

"There, now," Tulley said. "Don't get excited. You couldn't go, even if you wanted to. You're not able to make that ride."

At daybreak, urging the broncs on with yells, the night wrangler brought the remuda up from the flats and hazed it into the corral, hoofs pounding, horse bells clattering and dogs yelping excitedly. The hands began straggling up from the bunk-houses. They were all new men to Tulley except one, Cleon Jeffers, a rangy dark-haired man with a hawk-beak nose. By the time all of them had taken turns at the wash basins on the bench at the side of the cookshack, Tom Bradshaw appeared in the doorway and announced breakfast with bar and triangle. Tulley filed in with the others and stood near the door until all were seated. The nighthawk, having tied on an apron to help Bradshaw with the meal, pointed at a vacant place between Gil Jebb and Obie Sheppard, and Tulley sat down. There was still plenty of room at the table, but no more plates had been laid.

Obie said, "Frank, you sure made a believer out of Marie Simpson. How do you do it?"

"The best way to win a girl's confidence, Obie, is do something for her. Like taking a .44 slug through the leg, for instance."

Gil Jebb said, "It ain't a matter of confidence,

Obie. They're in the same boat over that Burk killing, and Marie's afraid Tulley will talk."

The curly-haired Obie leaned sideways to see past Tulley. "Tell me the rest of it, Gil, and maybe we can get Garth out of jail."

"The way to get Garth out of jail is let a good lawyer do it. That's the way the country's being run now. Besides, he's not in any danger," the foreman scoffed.

"He'd be safer at home."

The other hands around the table had their attention on Tulley, but there was no further conversation except that needed to summon the swamper with the coffeepot and to pass the beans and biscuits, steak and gravy, dried peaches and molasses.

Leaving the cookshack, the G Bar L hands scattered. Some headed for the far corral to harness the work teams and continue with the haying; others led their broncs to the blacksmith shed for horse-shoeing. Two of the hands were assigned the chore of taking the bows and sheet off the chuck wagon which had just come in from calf roundup, and some of the men were getting ready to load up pack horses and return to line camps where they were customarily stationed when calf roundup was over.

None of the men asked Tulley for details concerning his limp or his recent whereabouts. If he joined the outfit, there would be plenty of time to learn all about him, just by listening, and if he rode on, it wouldn't make any difference, anyway.

While the G Bar L headquarters were still in the shadow of the eastern ridge, Tulley helped with a bronc that had to be tied up before shoes could be tacked on it. Before he had finished with this, Gil Jebb came down from the office in the south end of the main bunkhouse and called him aside.

"Expect to join the outfit?"

"I told you how I felt about it."

Jebb nodded. "The reason for that is, you were foreman here yourself. Well, I'll tell you something—you can't just drift back here after five years and shove me out of this ramrod job. You're not entitled to it."

"You're not entitled to it, either, Jebb. When I was foreman here and somebody had to be ordered off of our range, I did the ordering. I didn't hide behind Garth. If you'd been holding up your end of things, Garth would be all right. He wouldn't be in jail now over that Jess Burk killing."

"Maybe not," Jebb said, "but *I* might be. I didn't hire out here to clear Garth Lenzie's title to the land he claims. That's a job for attorneys and courts and suchlike. If it can't be done from a saddle, I'm not qualified."

"Lawyers didn't help Garth fight the Kiowas and Comanches for this land," Tulley said.

"You did?"

"I sure as hell did."

Jebb's eyes glinted for a moment; then he went back toward the office, spurs dragging. Nettled, Tulley rejoined the hands at the blacksmith shed. He'd planned on riding over to Buffalo City today, but Bradshaw had asked him not to because of Marie Simpson. Curbing his impatience, Tulley kept busy, helping around the corrals and wherever he was needed, like a hand riding the chuckline. Two days passed, and on the morning of the third day, Bradshaw hunted him up and told him Marie wanted him.

Tulley had a rank growth of whiskers. Borrowing the cook's razor, strop, mug and brush and a piece of wrapping paper, he went around to the wash bench. His clothing was presentable. The G Bar L kept a supply of work clothes in stock, and any other time there would also have been a spare hat in the storeroom. Having scraped off the whiskers, Tulley was washing up when he heard horses on the Buffalo City road. He saw two men but recognized neither, and the riders kept on toward the ranch house.

Bradshaw stepped out of his doorway, saying, "That's Sheriff Ramage and Marie's daddy. Simpson sure took his time getting here. I sent him word about her day before yesterday."

Gil Jebb rode up to the ranch house as the sheriff and Mose Simpson dismounted, and the three went inside. By the time Tulley had finished with Bradshaw's shaving tools, the three had reappeared on the front gallery. Gil Jebb stepped back into his saddle and cantered down the slope. Pulling his horse to stop in front of the cook-shack, he swung down, asking, "Where's that girl, Tom?"

"Isn't she in the house?"

Jebb came toward the doorway, something in the cook's face having aroused his suspicion. "You know damned well she's not. You've cleaned your stuff out of that room. What did you do with her—where did you take her?"

"Never mind about that, Gil. She's my responsibility, not yours."

"But her folks are worried about her." The foreman gestured toward the men on the gallery. "The county sheriff is looking for her. Whose responsibility is that?"

"Not yours. You don't wear a badge."

"You don't, either. And I'm foreman of this ranch. I'm boss when Garth's not here. You don't see him around, do you?"

"You're not my boss," Bradshaw flared. "Since when can a foreman tell a cook what to do? I take my orders from the owner, and if you want to keep eating at my table, you'll get that through your head."

Putting a hand against Jebb's chest, Bradshaw shoved him back. Bradshaw kept pushing him backward toward his horse. The foreman's sharp features went livid. He whirled aside, drew his six-gun and lashed out with it, the gun barrel striking Bradshaw above the ear. Grunting, the cook went down.

He was up instantly, Jebb glaring at him. Holstering his six-shooter, Jebb strode toward the door again. He cut a look at Tulley, standing close, but Tulley did not move then. He waited until the foreman had planted one boot inside the cookshack; then he grabbed a fistful of Jebb's vest and hauled him backward.

Jebb was fast at snatching out his gun. He palmed it again while still off-balance. Grasping the foreman's wrist, Tulley bent his arm until the gun was pointed at Jebb's own mid-section.

"What are you doing, Tulley?"

"Trying to get you to show some sense, Gil."

"Give it to him, Frank!" Bradshaw cheered. "Run him plumb off this ranch!"

Jaws bulging with anger, the foreman continued to struggle.

"Go ahead," Tulley told him. "Shoot yourself in the guts. If I can get this hammer back, you really will shoot yourself, and the sheriff will think it was accidental."

Hoofbeats pounded on the slope.

Jebb turned loose of the gun, and Tulley released him. Sidling away, the foreman picked up his hat, dusting it, and Tulley rammed the man's six-shooter into its leather.

"Don't you ever pull that on Tom or me again."

"I was just trying to do right."

Sheriff Ramage had stopped his horse and dismounted. Tulley faced him. The lawman was a burly, square-shouldered man with a florid, jowled face and bright blue eyes under a low-crowned, silver-decorated Mexican sombrero. The silver star on his vest, Tulley observed, was twice the size of an ordinary law badge.

Ramage's gaze moved from one to another and settled on the foreman. "What's the ruckus about, Gil?"

Jebb was slow in replying.

Tulley said, "Just a misunderstanding, Sheriff, as to who's boss of the cookshack."

"And you had to take Gil's gun away from him. What was your put-in?"

Tulley gave Al Ramage a hard scrutiny. "I don't know. I just thought it would sound better to Garth if there wasn't any gunplay. Of course, if you figure there ought to be some, I can accommodate him."

"It looked to me like Gil was trying to go inside there, mister, and you and Tom Bradshaw didn't want him to."

Tulley kept quiet.

Mose Simpson, having dismounted, too, said, "Bradshaw, is my daughter in there?" In a loud tone, he called, "Marie, I've come for you. What did you run off for? Ain't you ashamed, here on this ranch with no womenfolks?"

Tulley said, "Simpson, Tom sent you word about her. You know she was hurt the other night. She hasn't been able to come home."

"I want to see her."

Bradshaw blocked the doorway. "I'm her doctor. If she doesn't want to see anyone, she doesn't have to. I think Frank Tulley will back me up in that."

Sheriff Ramage lifted his brows. "Doctor? Why in hell ain't you over in Buffalo City taking care of sick folks? I reckon you mean you're a horse doctor."

Bradshaw gave him a resentful stare.

"Go ask the girl what she wants to do. You don't know," the sheriff ordered.

Angered, Bradshaw stepped into the building and headed for his private quarters.

"Ramage," Tulley said, "I've had quite a bit of experience with sodbusters, here and there. Is Garth Lenzie safe in your jail?"

"I don't know. But if they get Garth, they'll have to swap for him. I gave Calico Thompson orders to shoot to kill if any lynch talk started."

Bradshaw returned, saying, "She'll talk with you. Go right on through the middle door."

Frank Tulley smoked a cigarette while he and Jebb and Bradshaw waited.

Ramage and Simpson were both poker-faced and silent when they came back outside and got back astride their horses. Slanting a look at the cook, Sheriff Ramage said, "She aims to stay a while, Bradshaw. Take good care of her. Me and Mose will explain it to her ma."

"Did she tell you what she was doing up there on our south-west range after dark?"

"If she did, do you think I might feel obligated to pass such information on to you?"

"No," Bradshaw said. He regarded the sheriff with intense dislike.

Ramage glanced at the girl's father. "Ready to ride, Mose?"

"Yes, sir."

Grave of mien, Simpson reined his horse around and touched it with his rowels—a big-shouldered, yellow-haired man in baggy store clothes. He kept a little behind Ramage as they took the Buffalo City road.

Chapter Four

Picking up the quarrel, Gil Jebb said to Frank Tulley, "You figure there's room for you and me both here?"

"That's up to you."

"I'm foreman of this ranch."

"Sure you are! What in hell are you bellyaching about?"

Bradshaw laughed.

Whirling about, Jebb stalked toward the office, and Tulley put his gaze on the men riding the Buffalo City road.

It was short-grass and mesquite range in that direction; undulating land, this side of Double Mountain. Pale-coloured longhorns grazed here and there in the sunshine—cattle that would have to be sold if Garth Lenzie was called upon to defend himself in court.

Bradshaw said, "I should have explained to Gil about Marie. Bringing her down here was the only way I could talk her into letting you go to Buffalo City."

Tulley started inside. "I put your razor here on this table, Tom."

Marie was wearing one of Katie's blue-and-white calico dresses that contrasted becomingly with her yellow hair. Her left arm was in a sling, and she was seated in an easy chair. It was her expression of fear and confusion that alarmed Frank Tulley. He placed the grey Stetson he'd borrowed from Bradshaw on the heavy bureau and moved a chair around to sit down facing Marie.

"Did you tell your father and the sheriff what the trouble was the other night?"

"I told Sheriff Ramage."

Tulley turned his gaze on the back door. It was ajar, and opened on to the smokehouse. "Mose waited out there while you talked to the sheriff?"

"Yes."

"Then you didn't want your father to know what you told Sheriff Ramage. You don't want me to know it, either?"

"No."

"What did you mean the other night when you said, 'Why did he unload it?' "

"I don't remember saying that." Her dainty features were strained with worry.

"You know what I think about you, Marie? You've just found out what a bunch of skunks the general run of people can be sometimes. You feel let down. What did you learn—that Jess Burk was a horse thief?"

She moistened her lips. "I don't want to talk about it, Tulley."

Tulley slapped his knee. "I'm going to head for town. If there's anything you want from your house, I can stop there."

“Tell Mother to keep Daddy at home. For him to watch out. And you be careful, Tulley. If anything happened to you, I—well, I would just die.”

Frank Tulley grinned. “If you want that the way it sounded, ma’am, I wouldn’t need to ride a horse over to Buffalo City. These boots would cover it in about six steps.”

“What about Katie Lenzie?”

Frank Tulley sobered, and presently he went back outside.

Bradshaw wasn’t outside, but Obie Sheppard and Cleon Jeffers were, obviously waiting for Tulley. The hawk-beaked Jeffers said, “We don’t know whether to take orders from Gil Jebb or Tom Bradshaw, but Tom told us to go with you.”

“Well, you have a choice, Cleon. If you want to help Garth, follow Tom’s orders.”

“Are you going to town?”

“As soon as I can saddle up.”

“Things are different here now, Frank,” Jeffers said seriously. “Buffalo City’s all tamed down. Let’s not try something we can’t get away with.”

“Why?”

Jeffers frowned, searching for an answer.

“It would be risky for Garth,” Obie Sheppard said.

“It’s risky for him anyway, Obie.”

They looked at each other. Abashed, Jeffers said, “You’re plumb right, Frank. Let’s get going.”

At the corral, they caught up horses and cinched on saddles. They got their carbines at the bunkhouse. When they emerged, Gil Jebb was watching them from the doorway of the office.

"Obie, I told you and Cleon to ride over to Barrel Springs and clean it out."

"We aim to, Gil, but we're going to town first."

The foreman shifted his gaze down across the range, then looking back, he said, "You fellows may be able to get Garth out of that jail, but you won't be helping him any. You'll be playing right into those farmers' hands. They'll declare open season on him, sure."

"We'll get him out of jail first," Sheppard said, "and worry about the clodhoppers afterward. But you're the boss, Gil. If you say stay here, I'll stay."

Jebb disapprovingly shook his head. "It ain't my time to say amen, Obie."

Climbing into their saddles, the three of them rode off. Tom Bradshaw watched them go, and wondered if he had made another mistake.

The freshness that had spread across the range with the rainfall a few days back was gone now, and heat devils shimmered before their eyes as they jogged toward town, trailing the dust raised by Sheriff Ramage and Marie's father.

The G Bar L remuda was scattered over the flat immediately below the ranch headquarters. Meadow larks whistled on all sides. Here and there hawks wheeled across the range, skimming low in quest of prey, and longhorn cows with calves sought the shade of the isolated mottes of trees.

Not wanting to close up on the men ahead, Tulley, Jeffers and Sheppard held their mounts to a slow pace. The horses gaunted, nevertheless, and they stopped to tighten cinches.

"Garth and Vince will need horses," Sheppard said. "Sheriff Ramage probably has theirs in the county corral under lock and key. What'll we do about that if we don't get the key?"

Jeffers said, "We'll tell that old cuss at the livery stable what we're up to, and have him saddle us a couple of his horses. If he hasn't got any, the ones Katie and Effie drove in aren't too bad. Of course, *they'd* be stuck in town then."

"Are you speaking of old Dave Hildebrand?" Tulley asked.

"Yeah," Jeffers said. "Dave's still there at the livery, Frank."

Far to the left stood the belt of timber along Yeguas Creek. Straight ahead, to the north-west, rose the knobs of Double Mountain. A hogback ridge blocked off sight of the lower declivities of those knobs. Having ridden through there countless times, however, Frank Tulley knew that this road entered the timber at that point to follow close to the stream. The road and the creek separated Double Mountain, and it was at this spot that Garth Lenzie was trying to stop the hoemen. None of the land south of Double Mountain had been put to the plough, and at this moment Frank Tulley vowed that it never would be. Locking Garth up was the final straw.

Topping out on the hogback finally, the three of them caught sight of the place where Jess Burk had been killed. Charred ruins of the home and outbuildings still stood.

Sheriff Ramage and Mose Simpson had stopped at the ruins, their ground-tied horses standing hip-shot with sagging girths near the skeletal barn.

"They're looking for something," Sheppard said. "Ramage came by here on the way up. He must be hunting something that Marie told him about."

"Her saddle, maybe," Tulley said. "She was riding that bronc bareback the other night."

"You think she was here when Burk was killed?" Jeffers asked.

"She might have been."

The half-burned house stood on the right side of the road. A hundred yards back of it was a grave, judging from the cross and the masses of wilted sunflowers and other blossoms strewn about.

Sheppard said as they rode on, "That house could be repaired. If Ramage wasn't here, I'd set the damn thing afire again, so it would burn plumb up."

The three kept going straight ahead until the road struck the creek. Following the windings of Yeguas Creek through the coolness of the timber, they came to the spot that had been Frank Tulley's favourite watering place in the old days. Stopping here, they loosened cinches and let their mounts drink sparingly. Afterward they lit cigarettes and before they were ready to ride on, they heard the clatter of horseshoes on the rocky road. Sheriff Ramage and Mose Simpson appeared among the trees.

"Headed for town?" Ramage asked.

Tulley said, "Uh-huh, but we're not in a hurry."

Ramage stopped his horse. He looked Tulley over closely, as though appraising him, as though remembering how Tulley had disarmed Gil Jebb. He spoke to all three of them.

"I may have to pin badges on you fellows when you hit town."

Jeffers' lip curled. "Ramage, after what you done to Garth and Vince, don't ask me for help."

The sheriff's face reddened. "Cleon, don't get proddy with me. I did what I had to do. Garth's been making talk about how he aimed to burn Burk out, and when it happened, public opinion forced me to come and get him."

Jeffers looked disgusted. "It wasn't public opinion, Ramage. It was Webb Colter."

Anger flared in Ramage's eyes. "I said it was public opinion! If you think you can do a better job than I'm doing, I'll see that you get the chance to, by God!"

"I've got a job," Jeffers growled. "I wouldn't hurt the G Bar L to be president of Texas."

Ramage looked disgusted. "That's just what I'd expect from a jughaid like you. Have you ever voted?"

"Voted? No."

Ramage twisted in the saddle to look at Simpson. "Let's go, Mose." They rode on.

Tulley said, "I expect wearing that sheriff star is a hard job, Cleon."

"I don't doubt that, but Ramage is too hard-headed."

"He said he might have to put badges on us, though, and that means he's on Garth's side," Tulley said, reflecting that all Jeffers could think of was that Ramage had locked Garth up. He and Sheppard and Jeffers loafed in the shade for half an hour longer before proceeding on toward Buffalo City.

Beyond Double Mountain the road veered away from the creek and was flanked on either side by a cornfield. When the field on the right ended, a nester layout of barn lot, dug well and log house hove into view. A team of black horses stood head to tail switching flies off each other, under a shade tree at the back of the lot, and a flock of white chickens lay in the shade of the barn.

No one was in sight, but a window curtain was

pushed aside, as if someone stood there watching the G Bar L men ride by.

Nesters spooked easily, Tulley reflected morosely, remembering his trail-driving experiences in Kansas, unless there was a mob of them with some hell-fire-and-brimstone preacher egging them on.

Perhaps, Tulley mused, he had made a mistake in ever leaving Yeguas Valley. He could have toughed it out without Katie somehow. He'd had to do it anyway, other places, and maybe he could have kept these clodhoppers under control. It was too late now to run them out of this lower valley, and it might be too late for Garth to hang on to the range above Double Mountain, even while holding deeds to the water holes.

The road climbed a long slope and dropped down into a draw. A tributary of Yeguas Creek meandered in from the east along the bottom of the draw, and it was there that Mose Simpson had settled. Sheppard and Jeffers had prepared Tulley for sight of a farmhouse standing where there had been only shade and water for G Bar L cows five years ago, but the Simpson place looked more like the home of a prideful man than Tulley had anticipated. Nestled among tall trees quite a way back from the Buffalo City road, it was painted white, while the fences and outbuildings were red. There was a well-tended look about it all, and Tulley told himself that Marie's father wasn't as shiftless and no-account as he appeared to be.

Hoofprints revealed that Sheriff Ramage had ridden up the Simpson lane with Mose and had come out again, headed for town.

Leaving Sheppard and Jeffers dismounted in the shade of an oak, Tulley reined his chunky bay toward the farmhouse, and a small woman with light-coloured hair and a pinched face came out on the porch. Tulley touched his hat brim.

"Are you Marie's ma?"

"What do you want?"

"Is your husband at home?"

"No, he's—" Mrs. Simpson broke off, flushing, finding herself unable to lie to this calm-eyed man. "Well, yes, he may be here, too, somewhere out back. Want me to call him?"

"No, ma'am. I'm Frank Tulley. We just followed your husband and Sheriff Ramage from the G Bar L. I'm the one who found your daughter and took her there."

Concern and worry touched Maudie Simpson's pinched features. "Yes, I know. Sheriff Ramage said Marie intended to stay there a few days. Now if she's not badly hurt, Mr. Tulley, I want that girl at home. She's too young to be—"

"You want her alive, though, don't you?"

Mrs. Simpson stared at him, eyes round.

"Why was Marie so far from home in the first place, Mrs. Simpson?"

“It had something to do with a horse. Jess Burk—that man who was killed and burned out—bought a team of horses from Mr. Colter and gave him a note. Jess couldn’t pay up when the note came due, and Mr. Colter sent some men up here to get the team. Marie was riding one of the horses. She wouldn’t give it up. She took off up through the woods on it. Then that dreadful thing happened up there—Jess Burk massacred, his buildings set on fire and people rushing past here to see about it. It was a terrible cloud of smoke before the rain set in. That’s why she was up there—she just wouldn’t give up Jess’s horse.”

“Who told you all that?”

“Mr. Simpson.”

“Was Marie at home here when they came for the team? You said she took off up through the woods.”

Maudie Simpson shook her head. “She was over across the creek, visiting relatives.”

Tulley’s eyes narrowed thoughtfully. Marie had mentioned nothing about a wagon team; she had only said Jess had bought the horse from Lige.

So Marie had told her mother she was going to visit relatives, when actually the girl had circled around and taken the road to Jess Burk’s place. Shifting in the saddle, Tulley slapped a palm with the rein ends.

“Marie had been planning to marry Jess, hadn’t she?”

"Why, goodness no! Mr. Simpson would have shot Jess Burk himself, before he would have let that happen."

"Maybe he did."

Maudie Simpson blinked. Voice thinning, she asked, "Are you saying my husband killed Jess Burk and burned his house down? Mose wouldn't do such a thing!"

"Was he here at home?"

"Yes, he was. He was right here every blessed minute."

"Well, I'm much obliged to you, ma'am," Tulley said. He touched his hat again and rode back to the road where Jeffers and Sheppard waited. Tulley frowned. Apparently Mose Simpson had gone into hiding. Tulley hadn't learned anything from his daughter, but he had learned plenty from Sheriff Ramage. Simpson knew things he shouldn't have known, if he had been at home the day of the killing.

Chapter Five

A few minutes' ride beyond the Simpson place brought the three G Bar L men to a branch road which went west. Tulley told himself this was the road Marie had taken before turning back to recross the stream somewhere near Double Mountain. He was almost certain that Marie had been at the Burk place at the time of the killing and knew the men who'd done it. If the killers had been Garth Lenzie and Vince Potter, Marie would have acted quite different about going to the G Bar L, and she wouldn't be staying there now. Therefore, Tulley reasoned, she had been trying to escape from the very men who'd slain Burk—Carnotte and Spaugh and Wessels. It was hard to believe that Lige Wessels would take part in something like that, though.

"If Ramage is in his office," Jeffers said as they jogged along, "we'll stick a gun in his ribs, march him back to the cells. We'll get Garth and Vince out, and lock Ramage in, and get gone."

"And if he's not there," Sheppard said, "we'll do old Calico Thompson the same way."

"All I'm interested in," Tulley said, "is getting Garth straddling a bronc and headed out of town. I don't care how we do it."

They passed buggies, buckboards and wagons

headed both ways as they rode on, but none of the hoemen appeared warlike. Darkness closed in before they reached the settlement. From the last hogback Tulley looked down on the lights of the town and found that they covered twice the territory of the old days. Lamplighted residences flanked the road on both sides from here on.

John Pemberton's wagon yard was a familiar sight to Tulley, and so were John's store and hotel. The stage station, express office and livery stable patronized by the G Bar L were on a cross street. Buffalo City was the westernmost settlement this side of New Mexico. Now, with thousands of people on the move seeking new homes and a decent life where everyone was equal, Tulley wasn't surprised to find the town filled with vehicles and saddle horses.

The plaza lay to the north-west of the principal intersection. A two-storey courthouse centred it now.

"Sheriff Ramage has this south half of the bottom floor," Sheppard said. "It'll be easy."

"Yonder's the Cowman's Ruin Saloon. How's that for a name, Frank?"

"Webb Colter's joint, huh?"

"He plays poker there. His office is here in the hotel."

Opposite the hotel on the street which ran east toward the livery stable lay Mexican-town, with a row of cantinas and fandango houses, noisy now with music from stringed instruments, clapping hands, stamping feet and banged bottles and glasses. Fragrant odours of cooking food and spilled pulque wafted forth to mingle with the smell of street dust. This part of town was the favourite haunt of the teamsters and bullwhackers and buffalo hunters, as well as of the *vaqueros* from the ranches in the valleys branching off from the Brazos.

A man came out of the stable office with a lantern when the G Bar L hands dismounted at the gate of the public corral. He was thick-set and grizzled, but square of shoulder and erect. A battered hat was pulled low on one bushy-browed eye. He wore range boots with no spurs and wasn't packing a gun.

Obie Sheppard said, "Where's Dave Hildebrand, Calico?"

"He's having a spell with his back and took to his bed," Calico Thompson said.

"Are you in charge here?"

"Well, I'm supposed to be over at the courthouse helping Al, but he didn't have nothing for me to do, so I told Dave I'd help him out here tonight. What do you fellers want?"

"Obie," Jeffers said warningly, "Calico is Ramage's right-hand man. We'd better make him understand how serious this is."

"Son, I don't savvy your lingo, but I'm exactly what I told Dave I'd be—the stableman here tonight. Deal with me as you would with him, and it won't go no further."

"If it does," Jeffers said, "you'll be bedridden a while, yourself."

"Don't threaten me, son. Now what is it you fellers are so touchy about? Act like you're about to hold up a candy store somewheres."

"Are you carrying the keys to the jail?" Sheppard asked.

"I hid them. And you ain't going to get them."

"Well, you feed our broncs a bait of oats and saddle us a couple of extra ones for Garth and Vince. We're going up the street to eat supper."

Calico Thompson set the lantern on a gate-post and opened the gate. "Take your nags on in."

A horse stood, hipshot, in the darkness, tied to the fence inside.

"Whose is that?" Tulley asked.

"Belongs to Hildebrand. A feller is renting it to do a little courting."

"If one of Dave's horses stops a slug," Sheppard said, "we'll pay you for it."

Calico Thompson stood silent, swinging the lantern to and fro. "I've got more sense than I thought I had. If I'd of been around the court-house tonight, you fellers might have plugged me."

"We don't intend to shoot anybody," Tulley said. "And you keep your lip buttoned, Calico."

"Why, sure. They're not my prisoners." Calico chuckled.

The G Bar L men washed up at the corral pump before walking back up town.

The veranda of the hotel was brightly lighted, and now there was a crowd around the steps and on the veranda itself. Mostly sodbusters. Their voices were angry, and it was Sheriff Al Ramage they were lambasting. A smaller group stood to one side of the lobby doorway and among the group was Vince Potter. When the G Bar L trio had ascended to the veranda, Jeffers stepped up to Potter and asked, "What's the matter with them, Vince?"

"They want to see me hang for something I didn't do, I reckon."

"What they're really going to see," Sheppard said, "is about a half-dozen of them walking on their own guts if they don't tuck their tails and get gone." He turned his back on the hoemen. "What happened, Vince? Did Ramage let you go and keep Garth locked up?"

Vince Potter was a rawboned waddy with sorrel hair and a freckled face, and he was really a free man, Tulley saw, for he was wearing his six-shooter.

Vince gestured at the lobby. "Garth's in yonder with Effie and Katie, eating supper." Then, addressing the nesters, he said, "You hoemen had better know for sure what you're doing. None of us G Bar L men had anything to do with killing Jess Burk, and we don't aim to be pushed around about it."

Obie Sheppard faced the group. "Which one of them is doing the pushing, Vince?"

"Nobody's trying to push him around," one of the sodbusters blazed. "We was just trying to find out why Ramage unlocked that jailhouse door on his own account. Fred Blake didn't know nothing about it."

Potter said, "Damn it, I don't, either!"

"Quit arguing, Vince." Jeffers took Potter by the arm, and the four of them moved among the Windsor chairs to the end of the veranda. Jeffers said then, "Me and Obie and Frank Tulley here came to town on purpose to get you and Garth out of that hoosegow."

"I knowed you'd be here. With or without Gil Jebb. Have you come back to be ramrod again, Tulley?"

"I'm packing too big a poke to work for anybody now, Vince. Maybe later."

Potter said, "That trail money's good, I hear. Well, right now I feel like celebrating. Let's all go up to Francisca's Place and drink one to Sheriff Ramage."

"Let's go to the Parlour," Jeffers suggested. "I owe Ben Mullins a pretty big bar bill and I don't want to be seen drinking anyone else's liquor."

They started off.

Sheppard said, “How about you, Frank? Ain’t you going?”

“I want to see Garth.”

Tulley watched as the three clanked their spurs down the veranda steps, Obie and Cleon having forgotten all about coming here to eat supper. They went across the street, passed John Pemberton’s general store and continued toward the source of the piano music. Ben Mullins’ Parlour Saloon.

Sheriff Ramage had released Garth and Vince immediately upon arriving back in town, without explaining why, at least to Potter. Had Ramage done so, Tulley wondered, because Marie had told him that she’d seen Carnotte—and maybe Wessels—kill Burk?

Then why had Marie talked only to the sheriff? Tulley asked himself. Well, that could have been because she’d been betrayed by someone she believed in, and was no longer certain whom she could trust. Likely, she was afraid of trying to determine who were friends of the men she’d been running from.

Moving among the men on the veranda, Tulley started into the lobby. As he did so, a man on the way out gave way, stopping abruptly. He was tall and well-built, attired in a broadcloth suit and checked vest. Under the broad white hat his hair was shiny black, thick but carefully barbered. A brush of black moustache showed on his upper lip and his dark eyes held a sardonic gleam. He didn't say anything. Tulley took only distant notice of him, not even thanking him, and he went on out.

The lobby was brightly lighted from an elaborate chandelier and wall lamps, as it had been ever since Ben Mullins opened it for business. The same heavy chairs and leather couches stood about, occupied by guests chatting and reading newspapers. Behind the desk in the stairway alcove stood the night clerk, an old friend.

"Who did I almost bump into, Walter?"

The clerk was cadaverous and grey, addicted to light clothing and pomade. "That was one of our guests and local businessmen—Mr. Webb Colter. Nice fellow. Good to see you, Frank, after all these years. Want a room?"

"Not now. I'm going back and eat."

A panelled divider blocked off sight of the dining room. Rounding it, Tulley removed the borrowed hat and hung it on one of the hooks under the antlered head. The dining room was spacious, with a well-scrubbed floor and panelled walls. Framed paintings hung here and there and on one wall was a Seth Thomas clock. There was a huge sideboard and thirty tables with four chairs each. Two blue-clad serving girls in frilly aprons were in attendance, and one stood near the Lenzie table, for the Lenzies were above suspicion of wrongdoing to the management of this hotel. The other girl, smiling a welcome, came toward Frank Tulley to seat him.

Garth had his back to Tulley. He was wolf-lean and gnarled, with a mane of iron-grey hair. Effie was quite a bit younger—she'd been only sixteen when Katie was born. At the moment she was round-faced and buxom and, as always, determined to have her own way. She wore her hair parted in the centre and brushed back, and sat on Garth's right.

Katie was facing him. A throwback to her grandparents, Katie was, for she was taller than either Effie or Garth. The years spent back East there had filled out her body as well as her mind, Frank Tulley noticed. She still had the same delicate, clean-cut, lovely features. Her hair was a rich brown, and her long-lashed eyes were brown, too.

Tulley took a chair facing the rear so he could look at her.

He had placed his order and the waitress had headed for the pantry before Katie gave him a blank impersonal stare, her head tilted sidewise. A tiny frown furrowed her brow. Recognition came; she dropped her gaze.

She was disconcerted, flushing, and it made Frank Tulley deeply thoughtful. Katie looked up at her father finally and said something. The old G Bar L rawhider twisted around in his chair.

"Frank Tulley, you on a high lonesome?"
"Not quite."
"Then come over here and say howdy."
Going among the other diners, Tulley shook hands with Garth, greeted Effie, and said to Katie, "Took you a mighty long time to recognize me."
Garth said, "Sit down there and order something, Frank," and Tulley took the chair across the table from Effie Lenzie. The old rawhider said then, "Katie was daydreaming."
"About what?"
"Dreaming up ways to help my enemies push me off the G Bar L."
"Katie wouldn't do that. She's trying to help you, and you just don't know it."
"Show Frank your ring, Katie."
In a low, angry tone, Katie said, "Oh, don't start that again."
Dropping his gaze, Frank caught the sparkle of the diamond solitaire. He fell silent. He began eating his roast beef.
Effie said, "What have you been doing the last few years, Frank?"
"Working for Reed Anthony lately," Tulley said. He told them about the cattle drive to New Mexico, choosing the more enjoyable incidents of it, and not mentioning the events of the night he had arrived back in Yeguas Valley. Nor did he mention taking Marie Simpson to the G Bar L. He didn't even explain that he had come to town

with Cleon and Obie to free Garth and Vince from the county jail.

Somehow, while talking, Tulley managed to eat a big meal, the Lenzies lingering over dessert and coffee. The four left the dining room together and paused at the foot of the lobby stairs.

Effie said, “Frank, did you know that Garth just got out of jail?”

“Yes, ma’am. I heard about that Jess Burk affair.”

“It sure had us worried. But we’ll be going home in the morning, thank goodness. Can you be ready by daylight?”

“Me?”

“Aren’t you going to take your old job back?”

“I can’t, Effie.”

She watched him gravely. “Why can’t you—afraid of the nesters?”

“You know better than that, Effie. But I’ve been gone five years. I can’t expect just to drift back in here and push Gil Jebb out of that job.”

Mrs. Lenzie’s eyes gleamed with stubbornness. “Frank Tulley, do you think Gil Jebb’s feelings are more important than my own self-respect? The G Bar L has fallen to staves without you. When I laid eyes on you a while ago, I told myself everything was going to be all right now. I could walk the streets of this town and hold my head up again.”

Katie said reproachfully, “Mama—”

"You keep quiet," Effie told her. Her tone caustic, she added, "Go on upstairs, Katie, and give your intended a sweet kiss before he leaves for his Cowman's Ruin Saloon." She looked back at Tulley. "We need you."

"I'll always be handy, Effie."

Mrs. Lenzie and her daughter went upstairs to their quarters.

Chapter Six

Garth Lenzie offered Frank Tulley a cigar, and Tulley took it. They moved to a couch in a corner of the almost-deserted lobby. Getting his cheroot lighted, the G Bar L owner puffed out a cloud of fragrant smoke and said, "How long have you been back, Frank?"

"I just came from the ranch, Garth—me and Cleon and Obie. Tom Bradshaw sent us over here to get you out of that jail."

Lenzie smoked in pleased silence; then murmured, "Best outfit I ever had."

Tulley felt a prickle of heat on his face, but there was nothing intentional in the remark, and Garth looked as if he didn't even know what he had said.

"Bradshaw told me that Colter has you forced to the wall. Tom figures Colter framed the Burk killing on you."

"Hell, he didn't have to frame it on me. I framed it on myself. By talking too much. If Colter was behind it, he was just taking advantage of an opportunity." Vehemently Lenzie said, "He must have been behind it. No one else had a reason to shoot Burk and burn his buildings."

"Was he shot?"

Lenzie cut a strained look at him. “Hell, I don’t know. I just supposed he was.”

“Mose Simpson had a reason for doing it, from what I hear,” Tulley said.

“Because of his daughter?” Lenzie shook his head. “Mose wouldn’t go that far, Frank. Besides, he wouldn’t have to. Now if they had slipped off and got married, Mose might of done it.” Another cloud of cigar smoke wafted across his face. “I’ve heard a right smart about that girl of Mose’s. She must be a looker.”

“Nice girl,” Tulley said. “Garth, it’s a cinch that the sheriff changed his mind about you. Did he explain?”

“No.”

“Ramage probably knows the whole deal now, Garth,” Tulley said. He explained about Wessels and Carnotte and Spaugh riding up to his campfire. He told about Marie Simpson and the horse, about Ramage and Simpson’s visit to the G Bar L headquarters.

“I noticed you had a game leg,” Lenzie said, “but I figured it was permanent and didn’t mention it.”

Silence fell between them.

“I did right in taking her there, didn’t I, Garth?”

“Why, sure. Anyone who’s hurt is welcome there.” Thoughtfully, he added, “That gal’s testimony might make a big difference to somebody. When I get home, I’d better put a cordon of my men around her. Are you sure them fellows was trying to kill her?"

"No. But I'm sure they were trying to kill me. Garth, if Webb Colter wanted to get shut of you, as Bradshaw says, it seems to me it would have been simpler to have had you bushwhacked, instead of taking a long chance on you being accused of the Burk killing."

"Webb don't want me dead. He wants to rob me. Fact is, when you come right down to it, I don't actually believe he had Burk killed. But I'm saying he did. Webb knows that I've mortgaged my cattle to raise money to buy land certificates with. Get my water holes legally recorded. The only way I can borrow money now is put up my deeded lands as collateral. Defending myself in court, I'd of had to do it. Then Webb would have got my water holes. Then the whole ranch."

"Would Katie marry Colter, knowing he was trying to rob you?"

"She's wearing his ring."

"I just don't savvy that at all," Tulley said feelingly.

Lenzie leaned forward to flick ash into a tall brass cuspidor. He straightened back on the couch and ran his gaze idly over the lobby.

"Progress, Frank—changing times. Katie says it's happening all over the West. The big ranches are done for, she says. Falling to the plough. She blames me for not staying on my toes, for not buying up that damned scrip when I could have got it for a song."

Tulley frowned. "What's Webb Colter's hurry? Marrying Katie, he'll own the G Bar L someday, anyway. He's got no call to take it away from you. That is, if he's really shooting square with Katie."

"Frank, my wife was thirty-eight years old her last birthday. It's Effie they're taking it from. Effie may outlast both of them, and she'll fight them as long as she draws breath."

Tulley slowly shook his head, and Garth sighed heavily. "Well, a man has to face up to the fact that when he starts getting old, somebody's going to try to tear hell out of his life's work. You take that—"

At this moment somewhere outside sounded three fast gunshots, with echoes that resounded among the buildings around the plaza. Hoofbeats pounded along the street. Tulley heard a remote shout.

"Somebody's celebrating, Frank. Reckon it's my boys?"

"I'll go see," Tulley said, "but that wasn't the right kind of a yell." He got up and left the lobby. Men were converging on the plaza in front of the lighted courthouse, and Tulley went that way, too, hearing someone shout, "Who is it?"

"Sheriff Ramage!" a man yelled back.

Tulley found himself in the centre of a crowd. Several men rushed out of the courthouse, and one hurried back inside for a lantern. A body was sprawled on the grass. When lantern light spilled across it, stunned silence gripped the onlookers. The man on the ground was Sheriff Ramage, the front of his shirt and vest soaked with blood. There was a splotch of it on his badge. Tulley hunkered down and felt for a heartbeat. He glanced up saying, “I think he’s dead.”

At the edge of the gathering an authoritative voice ordered the onlookers to stand aside. Others took it up. “Stand back, men.” “Get back.” “Let Marshal Aikens through.” Tulley straightened.

Aikens said, “Right through the heart, huh? Did he speak? Who reached him first?”

A man back toward the courthouse steps said, “I did, Horace. He didn’t make a sound.”

Aikens squatted beside the dead man, and presently said, “Didn’t even get his gun out. I always figured Al was running a sandy about how fast he was.”

Tulley said, “Maybe he wasn’t expecting it, Horace,” and the marshal quickly stood erect.

He was unusually tall but quite stooped. A black hat was tilted precariously on the back of his head, the crown telescoped flat. His face was long and narrow. He had a turned-up nose and thick-lidded eyes, and was smooth-shaven except for bushy sideburns which reached almost to a line with his fleshy lips. Despite the heat, he wore a square-cut black coat, and carried his gun in a shoulder holster. Before becoming marshal, he had been lookout man for Ben Mullins in the Parlour Saloon, and he had been a friend on whom Frank Tulley could depend.

He said, "Howdy there, Frank Tulley. Did you see who did this?"

"I was in the hotel lobby."

"Anyone see it?"

No one said anything.

The marshal said, "Now, I know that a horse tore out east at a dead run right after those shots sounded. Someone must have seen who was riding that bronc."

"If he went east," a burly hide-hunter stated, "he won't go far. He'll head up Yeguas Creek. Ramage turned those G Bar L men loose a while ago, and them farmers up there aim to see justice done about that Burk fellow."

A man silhouetted against the lights of the Cowman's Ruin Saloon said, "I'm a Yeguas Creek farmer, and I know that none of us shot the sheriff. We don't sneak around shooting folks."

"That's right," another declared loudly. "Don't accuse us settlers of killing Al Ramage. We liked him."

Marshal Aikens said, "It appears to me that you clodhoppers are yelling mighty damned loud. I'd better not catch any of you packing a fouled gun barrel." He motioned at the men nearby. "Let's carry Al into his office."

Ready hands reached for the body of the sheriff, Frank Tulley helping.

"Hold on, Frank," Aikens said, "I want to talk with you," and Tulley stepped back.

The man with the lantern led the way into the courthouse, some of the crowd following. Others dispersed toward the places they'd been before the gunshots brought them onto the plaza.

The marshal turned to Tulley. "Are you going back to work as foreman of the G Bar L?"

"I'm not sure, Horace."

"I wouldn't do it if I were you."

"Well, I haven't really decided yet."

At this moment a man on the courthouse steps said, "Horace, who are you going to send after the man who shot Al Ramage?"

"I'm going to send you, Fred."

After a silence, the man said, "Ah, don't do me that way, Horace."

"I'm town marshal, Fred. That's a county job. I don't have any money to run a fugitive down with, and wouldn't have the authority to do it anyway."

"Who will they appoint now?"

"I don't know," Aikens said, and the man on the steps went into the courthouse.

"That's Fred Blake, the county attorney," Aikens said to Tulley.

"Sounded like he was shaking in his boots," Tulley commented.

Aikens was silent, standing on spread heels, chin lowered. Looking up finally, he said, "I'm going to be busy for a while, Frank. Will you come to the office in about an hour?"

"I'll be there," Tulley said, and the marshal went toward the group on the courthouse steps.

Tulley fell in with some men headed toward the Parlour Saloon. The piano music had stilled inside, and from the talk among the men with him, Tulley gathered that the piano player had gotten too drunk to hit the right keys. Al Ramage was already forgotten by these men. Obie and Cleon and Vince hadn't even showed up. Garth hadn't, either. Tulley could understand that, though. All the G Bar L men were in a mood to dodge the scene of trouble, because of Garth's narrow brush with prison or a noose.

It was all part of the same scheme. Sheriff Ramage had been shot for what Marie Simpson had told him about the Burk killing. Or, more likely, for the manner in which he planned to use that information. His releasing Garth and Vince proved that, in Frank Tulley's mind, at least.

An hour later when Tulley came back across the plaza toward Marshal Aikens' office, the area in front of the courthouse was deserted and the sheriff's office darkened. Ramage's body, he decided, had probably been moved to the undertaking establishment in the rear of the furniture store.

A drugstore stood on the north-east corner. The building west of that one was the marshal's office, a frame structure with a porch and wooden awning.

Tulley expected to find Aikens alone. In chairs drawn back from the table occupying the middle of the room, three other men lounged comfortably, filling the air under the hanging lamps with tobacco smoke. The marshal's desk stood against the east wall. Aikens was seated in his reversed swivel chair. Tulley knew the other men, and shook hands with them.

Aikens said, "Ben and John and George are the first commissioners of our new county, Frank, and they want you to bring in the man who beat Al Ramage to the draw."

"You figure he did?"

"Al was shot at close range. He had the best pair of eyes in the country. What do you think?"

"I think he knew who killed him, and didn't expect it."

"It could have been Webb Colter," Aikens murmured.

Tulley looked from one to another of the other men. John Pemberton was slight of build, grey and balding, with sunken cheeks and shrewd eyes. He was not only the owner of the biggest general store in western Texas, but he also operated his own wagon yard and freighting business, buying buffalo hides and sending them to railhead.

George Bankston was a blacksmith, a burly, sandy-headed man with a square chin.

Ben Mullins, hotel and saloon-owner, was a ponderous man with a double chin.

"They want to appoint you to finish out Ramage's term as sheriff," Aikens said. "Al's deputy resigned about a month ago, and Al couldn't find anyone else to take the badge."

"I thought Calico Thompson was his deputy."

"Just a handyman."

"It's a dangerous, thankless job," Aikens continued, "and nobody wants it."

Tulley said, "Why don't you be sheriff, Horace?"

"I'd be out of town too much. I'm needed right here. Town-tamers are harder to come by than sheriffs, Frank, and my job pays a lot more money."

Tulley nodded. "Will you give me a little time to think it over?"

"Can't. Come morning, Webb Colter will bring in his man to be appointed. If you're already wearing the star, these fellows won't have to tell Colter no."

"Is that so hard to do?"

"Not for me. Or you maybe. But if John Pemberton, there, told him no, it might cost John thousands of dollars. Colter's family is powerful back in St. Louis, where the big money is. Where John's wholesalers are."

"That's the way Colter plays, huh?"

Aikens nodded. “Take Ben, there,” he continued presently. “Colter wanted part of Ben’s hotel for his office, and Ben didn’t want to let him have it. They had a cuss fight, and Colter started up the Cowman’s Ruin Saloon to compete with Ben’s Parlour. Took a lot of your business, too, didn’t he, Ben?”

The elephantine saloon keeper nodded.

“There’s one other thing you’ll have to consider, Frank,” the marshal went on. “Al Ramage didn’t have the authority to turn Garth Lenzie out of jail. Fred Blake didn’t even know about it. So you’ll have to take Lenzie and Potter into custody again.”

Frank Tulley shook his head. “I wouldn’t do that. I’ll pass. Give your badge to someone else.”

Marshal Aikens shifted his gaze to the commissioners. “You’ll have to. We can see that Frank would play favourites if he was sheriff.”

They all got to their feet then, and Frank Tulley left.

Chapter Seven

When Frank Tulley went to the hotel to rent a room, he experienced a sensation of being spied upon, of being followed. Leaving the hotel, he was almost certain that hostile eyes were upon him from somewhere in the darkness, and he half-expected to be shot down, as Al Ramage had been.

Walking east, Tulley passed the stage station and express office, the revelry of Mexican-town loud on his left, the tempting odours of the cooking there rank in the night air. Adobe *casitas* stood across the street from the stable. Farther on, both sides of this thoroughfare were lined with such residences. At the edge of town this street became the stagecoach route to Fort Griffin as well as the road to the ranches over in the next valley.

Calico Thompson was seated on the threshold of the stable office, boots on the stoop, paring his nails with a penknife which hung from a chain fastened into a buttonhole of his vest. Tulley walked into the light from the doorway and stopped.

"Did Cleon and Obie tell you we wouldn't need those spare broncs?"

Calico Thompson's voice was subdued. "Yes,

they came. I didn't saddle any horses for you fellers. I just unsaddled yours. I knowed that Garth and Vince were already out of jail."

"Did you know that Ramage was going to get killed because of it?"

"Well, I knowed Al was wading in pretty deep. He was a good feller, but that star had gone to his head. He bawled out his backer in the Cowman's Ruin."

"Webb Colter?"

"Uh-huh."

"That why Dave Hildebrand got sick and you had to take his place here?"

"Uh-huh."

"Did the man show up to get the horse that was tied to the fence?"

"Yeah. And I reckon that's one mustang Hildebrand is going to lose. I sure hate to tell him about it."

"What are you talking about?" Tulley asked, hunkering down.

Calico Thompson stopped paring his nails and reared back. "I'm pretty sure Lige Wessels hightailed that horse yonderly. The lying skunk, he told me he was courting a sodbuster woman over across the creek and they aimed to go riding. But he didn't want to rent that bronc for no woman. He wanted it to make a getaway on."

"You think he killed Sheriff Ramage?"

"Well, he had the horse tied up here. He came

and got it. About a half-hour later I heard three gunshots. Then Lige lit a shuck out of here toward Fort Griffin. What else can a man think?"

"But why would he rent a horse, Calico?"

"He probably had one of his own horses loaded down for a long trail, and didn't want to be seen forking it in the middle of town. So he got one from me. I'd say that Lige's horses are valuable animals. He's right fond of the broncs he works with. And he figured Al Ramage would shoot back at him, maybe kill the horse he was straddling. If that had happened to his own horse, Lige would have had to grab one from a hitch-rail. That would have put an outfit of cowhands or *vaqueros* on his trail. And he knows too well what they'll do to a horse thief."

Tulley pulled out the makings. "It could have been like that, Calico, but Lige Wessels never would have guts enough to ride up to Al Ramage and shoot him down."

The oldster watched Tulley light the cigarette. He asked then, "Was you stove up by a bronc?"

"Bullet," Tulley said. "It's almost well."

Calico closed the penknife. "I'll tell you what was wrong with Al Ramage, Tulley. He was a deputy sheriff back yonder in East Texas where a law star carried a lot of weight. Once he got that star pinned on him, he figured he was boss-man of this county. He was, too, while he lasted. He took a posse up there to the G Bar L, and damned few badge-toters could have got by with it. Took more guts to do that than to go alone."

"Yeah. If Wessels turned that horse loose, Calico, would it come back here?"

"It might," Calico said. "Son, my idea is that Wessels knowed all about that Burk killing without taking part in it, and he had to shoot Al in order to keep his notches even with Carnotte's and Spaugh's."

"Do you know that to be a fact, Calico, or are you just speculating?"

"Just speculating, son."

Tulley stood erect. He finished the cigarette and tossed it into the street. Taking leave of Calico Thompson, he angled toward the *cantinas* and fandango houses, around the fronts of which were gathered *vaqueros* from ranches in nearby valleys.

Francisca's Place was a low-roofed but spacious adobe, lighted by green-shaded hanging lamps. Two bartenders were on duty behind the brass-railed mahogany. There were no games. No tables occupied the front part of the room, but chairs stood against the wall there. One contained a Mexican youth who dozed with a red sash around his middle and a guitar across his lap. One of the tables in the first row was flanked by empty chairs. Frank Tulley went to it and sat down, putting his back to the wall.

Three young *Mexicanas* circulated among the patrons. One of them, a slim and dark-eyed *señorita* in a red skirt and white blouse, came toward Tulley's table, swinging her hips.

"*Si, señor*?"

"Howdy. Are you Francisca?"

"*Si, señor.*"

Tulley laid a double eagle on the green baize tablecloth. "Bring me a bottle of tequila."

The girl took the money. She brought a square black bottle of liquor and a *trago* glass from the bar. When she put down the change, Tulley picked up only part of it.

"That's yours," he said, "if you'll tell me what that girl's name is." He indicated one of the other *señoritas*.

A smile flashed through this slim *señorita*'s eyes and across her lips. She only shrugged.

"Take it," Tulley said. "You're all Francisca. I used to live here."

Two more musicians entered the *cantina* now, one with a violin and the other with a guitar. The one with the guitar was strumming his instrument tentatively. Keeping a watch on the street doorway, noticing the men who came and went through it, Tulley filled his glass and picked up the salt cellar. He fisted his left hand and sprinkled some of the salt in the crotch of his thumb and forefinger. Touching his tongue to the salt, he tossed off the tequila.

At this moment the musicians broke into a lively Mexican dance, and the dark-eyed *señorita* who had served Tulley whirled on to the dance floor, heels tapping rhythmically. Red skirt swirling high to expose beautiful legs, she finished her dance to the roar of applause from the customers. A shower of coins spun on to the floor around her. Tulley downed another glass of tequila.

When the musicians began playing again, he saw a young *vaquero* leave the bar to approach the girl on the dance floor. Sweeping off his sombrero, the *vaquero* laid it at the girl's feet, and the two of them danced the *jarabe*, the *vaquero*'s spurs jingling in time to the *señorita*'s tapping high heels. She danced a circle around the hat and sank to one knee. The *vaquero* swung a boot above her head. He then spun the girl to her feet, ending the dance amid shouts of approval and banging of bottles and glasses on bar and table-top.

Frank Tulley was interested in something else now, however.

He'd seen the black-garbed, spade-bearded Jules Carnotte come through the front door. As though already informed of Tulley's whereabouts, Carnotte came straight toward the table. At this moment Griff Spaugh appeared. He had entered the bar-room from the rear. He, too, came toward Tulley's table, and he was carrying an extra hat.

The pair stood side by side in front of Tulley, and Spaugh held out the hat. It was a broad-brimmed white hat with a furred hole through the crown.

"Do you want this," Spaugh asked, "or would you rather have the money for it?"

"I'll take the hat."

Spaugh put it on the table.

Thumbs hooked in the belt that encircled his potbelly, the short-built Carnotte said, "Mind if we sit down? We want to palaver with you."

"Trying to weasel out of a showdown?"

The two pulled back chairs and seated themselves.

Spaugh said, "We had a right to be sore at you, Tulley. When we came up there to your camp, we never bothered you. But you took chips in our game. You kept us from catching that girl."

"You weren't trying to catch her. You were trying to kill her. That makes it everyone's business, Red."

"Who said we was trying to kill her?" Spaugh demanded. "We just shot at her to scare her. Trying to make her stop."

Tulley watched them with repressed anger.

"I'm right sorry I burned your stuff," Spaugh said. "But I was cussed mad. We had orders to bring that horse back to town. Every time we got within yelling distance of that split-tail, though, she drummed on that bronc's ribs. Wouldn't you have got mad, too?"

"No."

Carnotte exposed a fistful of coins. "We'll pay you for the damage. Will a couple of double eagles square it?"

"It would if it wasn't for this game leg. If a man ever tries to kill me once, I never forget it."

Griff Spaugh sneered. "You're a regular bad-man."

"When I have to be, yes. I learned a long time ago that the only thing that'll stampede a snake is another snake." Reaching for his tequila, Tulley poured another drink and downed it with a taste of salt.

Carnotte said, "We don't like you worth a damn, Tulley, but we've got orders to get along with you."

"Orders from who—Webb Colter?"

Carnotte and Spaugh exchanged a quick look, and Carnotte said, "Yeah."

"Taking a fair view of it," Spaugh said presently, "you didn't ask for chips in our game. You was dragged into it. Actually, you haven't got anything against us, or us against you, because we're here to pay you for what we done."

"How about the blood I lost?"

"Lige Wessels did that. I was shooting high," Spaugh said.

"Me, too," Carnotte said. "Do you think we

would of picked up your hat and brought it to you if we'd been trying to kill you?"

"Where is Lige Wessels?"

"He's gone for good."

"Dead?"

"No, not dead—he lit a shuck out of here. Aims to keep going."

Tulley gave his head a jerk. "You're just using this hat as an excuse. You hunted me up for some other reason."

"We told you," Carnotte said. "We're supposed to get along with you."

"Best way to do that is to cross the street ever'time you see me coming."

Spaugh began to look worried. "Be reasonable, Tulley. You could have been hit by a ricochet, you know."

"I'm thinking of Jess Burk," Tulley said. "You two murdered him."

"Was he kinfolks of yers?" Spaugh asked.

"No. But Garth Lenzie may be sometime, and he was put in jail for what you did."

Spaugh licked his lips. He was watching Tulley pour another *trago* of tequila. Carnotte, too, was being tormented by thirst, and Tulley reasoned that they had orders to lay off the liquor. Tulley sipped his slowly.

He said then, "Marie was in Jess Burk's barn when she saw you fellows coming, and when you set the barn afire, she made a run for it bareback. I saw Ramage trying to find her burned saddle."

"What else did she tell you?" Spaugh asked.

"She didn't tell me who was going to kill Al Ramage."

Carnotte said, "Lige did that."

"But if Al Ramage had played the game square," Spaugh said, "Lige wouldn't have done it. Ramage double-crossed the man who put him in office. Wouldn't follow orders. Hell, he wanted to give the orders."

"And Webb Colter wouldn't stand for that."

Spaugh shook his head.

"I reckon Colter told you fellows not to drink tonight, too, didn't he? You must be scared of him," Tulley jeered.

Carnotte and Spaugh ignored that.

"Colter sure goes all out to back up his gunmen," Tulley said. "Any man who'll have a sheriff killed to keep him from talking is treacherous. He'll do anything. Better not trust Webb Colter too far."

"You just keep cussing Colter," Spaugh said, "and see if we care."

Carnotte licked his lips. "How about some of that tequila, Tulley?"

"I never drink with a man I aim to kill."

"Hell, I'm going to have a drink," Carnotte muttered angrily. He twisted around in his chair and summoned one of the girls. He ordered a bottle of whisky. When the *señorita* brought it and he'd paid for it, he pulled the cork with his teeth and sloshed it into his parched throat directly from the bottle. He offered his partner some then.

"I don't want any," Spaugh said.

Leaning on his arms, Carnotte looked at Tulley. "You thinking about killing me?"

Tulley nodded. "I'm thinking about watching you hang."

Carnotte's spade-bearded face formed a sneer. "You've got my permission."

"You listen to me," Tulley said. "Up there on the G Bar L range after dark, you might have got by with shooting Marie. If anything happens to her now, or to Mose, either, I'll kill you both. I'll scalp you. I'll hold a scalp dance right down there on the plaza and invite the whole damned valley."

Jules Carnotte guffawed.

Chapter Eight

Marshal Aikens entered Francisca's Place as Carnotte's laughter died away. Black hat canted on the back of his long head, hands in the pockets of his coat, Aikens passed a look over the men at the bar. He moved his gaze slowly over those at the tables. His tall, stooped figure moving with snakelike grace, he came over near Frank Tulley and looked down at Jules Carnotte.

"What are you tickled about?"

"Nothing," Carnotte said. He was cold sober now.

Aikens looked at Tulley. "Both of those bottles yours, Frank?"

"No. The tequila's mine. Help yourself, Horace."

"I'll wait," the marshal said. He moved away. He walked to the rear of the room and sat down at a table with two *ganaderos* from over in the next valley.

Lowering his tone, Griff Spaugh said, "Tulley, you don't need to worry about Marie. She's got sense. When she hears about Ramage being dead, she'll understand it. She won't want her pa killed, too."

"She'll do what Colter tells her to, huh?"

"Sure."

Tulley said, "When she takes the witness stand, she'll swear she saw Garth and Vince kill Burk?"

Spaugh nodded.

"She won't be taking the witness stand."

Spaugh said, "Oh, yes, she will."

Tulley indicated the whisky. "Take that and get to hell away from here. There's other tables."

Pale eyes mean, the redheaded Spaugh pushed back his chair. "Come on, Jules," he said, and they went out through the front, taking along the unfinished bottle but leaving the extra hat on the table.

In the rear of the room Marshal Aikens took leave of the *ganaderos* and came up to Tulley's table. He sat down where Spaugh had been. "Did you settle it about the bushwhacking?" he asked, indicating the hat.

"About the hat, yes. Did you send them to me?"

"They came to town the other day with a wild tale about being jumped by a bushwhacker, and had this hat with them. A while ago they pointed you out as the man who'd shot at them, as owner of this hat. I told them that whatever happened up there in that hoot-owl country was somebody else's worry, not mine. I told them I'd pow-wow with you if it was me."

Tulley had thought that fear of reprisal had brought Spaugh and Carnotte to him. Now he felt let down, but he only nodded and said, "Help yourself to the tequila, Horace."

"Well, a little one won't do any harm," Aikens said.

At this moment the musicians struck up the old tune known as *La Cucuracha*, and Frank Tulley became interested in his surroundings, hoping to see the leggy *señorita* dance again. She didn't, though. Like the other two, she passed among the customers, making herself agreeable to all, while the bartenders hurried back and forth, filling the gullets of the drought-stricken men who came and went.

Frank Tulley's mind had changed itself, it seemed, for he found himself asking, "Horace, is Ramage's job still open?"

Aikens nodded. "On the same terms—that you lock Garth Lenzie up again. Fred Blake will insist on that."

"If it's part of the job, I'll do it."

The marshal's tone hardened. "Don't tell me something you don't aim to do."

"Have I ever done that?"

"No, but I've never really known you, Frank. As ramrod of the G Bar L, you had everything your own way. The G Bar L was a kingdom in them days. It's different now. Wearing a law badge is different, too. You can't swagger around with a go-to-hell attitude just because you're fast with a gun."

"Have I been doing that?"

Aikens nodded.

"Well, I sure didn't mean to," Tulley said.

Aikens took more of the tequila. "As sheriff, you'll have to soft-soap folks, Frank, and forget your friends. What I mean is, getting down to brass tacks, if you take the job, the G Bar L is going to toe the line. That outfit can't ride roughshod over everybody just because you was one of them."

"No, they can't do that. I'll play it down the middle."

Aikens showed his teeth. "Nobody can play it down the middle, Frank, but I'm willing for you to try. Come on. Let's go roust out the commissioners again."

Marshal Aikens and Frank Tulley left the revelry of Francisca's Place then, Tulley carrying along the extra hat and heading for his hotel room.

Tulley had the dead Ramage's oversized star pinned to his vest when he and Aikens relit the lamps in the sheriff's office.

There was one large office with two desks and chairs and a heavy table. There was a rack of rifles and shotguns, and back of the main office was a room containing two bunks. A corridor led to the rear of the building, and here a crosswise hall ran south in front of the cell block, which faced the back of the building.

Marshal Aikens said, “I use this lockup, too, but the town feeds my prisoners. You won’t have to bother with them.”

“You use any particular cell?”

“No.”

“They’re all empty now,” Tulley observed.

“They won’t be, though, when you go get Garth Lenzie.”

Tulley gave the marshal a quick look.

Thick-lidded eyes sharpening, Aikens said, “He’s still over at the hotel, not planning on leaving till daylight.”

“Do you have your own keys?” Tulley asked.

“Yes, to these cells. They never lock the building.”

Tulley turned into the corridor.

“Where are you going?” Aikens asked.

“To see about that warrant.”

John Pemberton had given Tulley a ring of keys. He sorted out one for the desk and unlocked the drawers and roll-top. He and Aikens both thumbed through the documents in the pigeonholes. Aikens found the warrants for Lenzie and Potter.

Slapping them down on the desk, he said, “There they are. When you serve them and turn a key on those fellows, you’re on your own as sheriff. Unless you call on me for help.”

“Well, I won’t need any warrants. They’ll take my word for it. I’ll go over after a while and see if Garth’s gone to bed.”

"See if he's gone to bed? By God, you'd better bring him back with you!"

Tulley backed away a few steps. "What do you mean by 'better,' Horace?"

Aikens appeared chagrined. "Well, Frank, I recommended you and I want to see you make good. Whatever you do is going to reflect on me, to a certain extent. Are you too damned important to be reminded of what you promised now that you're wearing that star?" Aikens had adopted his customary stance, legs spread, fingers gripping the lapel of his coat near the butt of his shoulder-holstered gun.

Tulley said, "You're drunk, Horace. You hit that tequila too heavy."

"Looking for trouble, Frank?"

"No, but you are. I savvy you, Horace. You've got this town and county under your thumb, judging from the way the commissioners jump to do your bidding. But I won't jump. If you recommended me for this star, expecting me to, you made a mistake. A big one."

Aikens stood motionless, his long sideburned visage enigmatic in the lamplight.

"Call the turn," Tulley said tensely.

"Well, Frank, you used to consider yourself a part of the Lenzie family. You may still consider that. I've had enough experience to know that when a girl gets into a man's blood he never actually gets entirely clear of her again as long as he lives. I'm betting that when the G Bar L chips are down, your gun will be down, too."

"Katie's engaged to marry Webb Colter."

"She don't know Webb like I do."

"Is he already married?"

"No."

Tulley pulled the swivel chair around to seat himself at the desk. "I'll lock Garth Lenzie up, like I said I would."

"If you don't," Aikens said, "we may have another short talk about it."

Thoroughly angry, Tulley kept his mouth shut. With the marshal looking on, he examined the contents of the desk drawers, searching for a deputy's badge. He found one and slipped it into his vest.

"Got someone in mind?" Aikens asked.

"No, but I will have."

"Hope it's not a G Bar L man," Aikens said unctuously. "Well, Frank, it's time for me to make another round of the deadfalls. Need help, call on me. Want advice, see the commissioners."

Tulley said, "I don't know whether I can make a hand here or not."

After Aikens had gone, he examined the papers that Ramage had collected more carefully, hoping to find something bearing on the land-scrip fight between Garth Lenzie and Webb Colter, something that would help Lenzie. There was nothing. A stack of "Wanted" dodgers caught his interest then, and he leafed through it. Even as he did so, however, he knew he wouldn't go out of his way to apprehend any of the wanted men. Western sheriffs didn't perform their duties in any such manner. If a man behaved himself here, he was safe from his past, criminal or not. Here, a man was accorded exactly what he—and those before him—had come to the West for: the chance to begin again.

Yet Frank Tulley had long suspected that Horace Aikens was afraid of his own backtrail, and now that Tulley had an opportunity to find out, he intended to do so.

There was nothing whatever in the desk concerning Aikens.

Well, Tulley told himself glumly, he'd better get a move on, go get Garth and lock him up, because Horace Aikens would be back here pretty soon.

Leaving the lamps burning but locking the door to his office, Tulley stood on the courthouse steps for a time looking over the still lively town, the liveliest spot of all seeming to be the Cowman's Ruin Saloon. His head filled with plans for ruining Garth Lenzie, the only cowman in the valley, Webb Colter had doubtless gotten a laugh out of naming that place. Or maybe he had done it to please the sodbusters. At any rate, to all who savvied the cow that name was a taunt, and Frank Tulley, himself, was resentful as he angled across the plaza.

Most of the Windsor chairs on the lamplighted hotel veranda were occupied by guests taking advantage of the cooler air outside. None of them said anything directly to Tulley, but as he went on into the lobby he was followed by the low-toned comment: "They say he accused Jules and Griff of killing Burk, in Francisca's Place a while ago," and Tulley knew then that the three of them had talked much louder than they had meant to talk.

Except for a shaggy oldster dozing on the sofa directly under the blazing chandelier, the lobby was deserted, but the night clerk was still behind the desk.

"Congratulations, Frank."

"You sure keep up with what's going on," Tulley said. "What room is Garth Lenzie in?"

"Rooms two and four and the front sitting room."

"Where's Webb Colter located?"

"Rooms one and three and five. His office opens into the centre room that the Lenzies are using. I mean, there's a door. It's locked now, of course."

"Is Colter up there now?"

The clerk briefly bowed his pomaded head. "I don't remember. He's probably at the Cowman's Ruin. I heard him mention a big poker game."

Tulley started to leave the desk, but the clerk stopped him. "I'm glad to see you wearing that star, Frank. I make mistakes, but I do my best, and I'm always on the side of law and order."

"You've got that kind of a reputation, Walter. But what are you getting at?"

"Well, if you make trouble for Mr. Colter, he'll just turn around and take it out on Ben Mullins."

"Go easy, eh?"

"Sure. Unless you want to wind up in the same shape as Al Ramage."

"You let me worry about that," Tulley said. He turned to the stairway, climbing with jingling spurs.

The upstairs hall was dimly lighted. Tulley was already familiar with the layout of the rooms. Seeing that the transom over the door of the centre room at the front was lamplighted, he rapped on it softly. Effie Lenzie opened it. She started to speak, but when she noticed his star, she almost slammed the door in Tulley's face, her own face becoming cold and resentful.

"Let me see Garth, Effie."

"He's not here."

"Yes, I am, too, Frank. Come on in."

Lenzie was seated in a huge rocker with his legs on an ottoman, and he didn't rise.

Slanting a look at him, Tulley said, "I need your co-operation, Garth."

"How so?"

Effie tapped the air with a forefinger in the direction of Tulley's star and said bitterly, "No wonder you weren't interested in your old job."

Garth said, "Effie, Al Ramage wasn't even dead when you was talking with Frank."

"Oh, that's right," Effie said contritely. "Won't you sit down, Frank?"

Tulley crossed the room and tossed his hat—his own—on to the rug at the end of the sofa.

Chapter Nine

Frank Tulley felt a little queasy as he sat down on the sofa because that put the back of his head to a window, and the curtains weren't drawn. The door to the room on his right, Colter's office, as the clerk had said, was closed. The door on the left stood ajar on a bedroom—Garth and Effie's obviously. Another door in that bedroom opened into the room Katie was using, and Katie's other door gave into the hallway. She had heard Tulley and knew he was here.

Mrs. Lenzie moved around to stand behind her husband's chair, appearing more like a daughter than a wife.

Garth said, "You're finishing out Ramage's term?"

Tulley nodded. "Ramage was killed, Garth, because he turned you and Vince Potter loose. When I put this star on, I promised to lock you up again."

"What?" Effie cried.

Garth threw his leonine old head back, watching Tulley with glinting eyes.

Tulley said, "Wait until you can see both sides of it before you decide."

"Decide what?" Effie asked.

"Whether I'm right or wrong."

Carefully, cautiously, Tulley recounted events

since the night he had built the campfire to cook the venison in the upper end of the valley. He told of refusing at first to accept the sheriff's star, but had decided that the killing of Jess Burk was only the first of several that were inevitable in this valley. He said, "You'll just have to trust me, Garth."

Lenzie shook his head stubbornly. "I'm not going back to jail. Something might happen to you, and I'd be a gone goose. I trust you, Frank, but I don't trust that Simpson gal. Her folks have never known anything but grubbing in the dirt for a living. Her sympathies are with her own kind. She was born to hate us cowmen, and if she could get rid of me, she would figure it a feather in her cap."

"You're wrong, Garth. Both about Marie and about going back to jail. You are going."

Effie had moved around to the escritoire. She opened a glass door which protected the bookshelves. A six-shooter lay on the bottom shelf, and she took it. She cocked it, the menacing sound catching the attention of both men. She stood there with it pointed at the ceiling, her round face flushed, her lips tightly compressed. Tulley ignored her.

He said to Garth, "I'll let you hide your gun in the cell. And if something happens to me, you'll have a chance to free yourself. What more can you ask?"

Effie said, "Don't pay any mind to him, Garth. I didn't even want you to let Al Ramage arrest you."

"No," the old rawhider said, "I'm not going to jail."

Effie said, "You go down to that Parlour Saloon, Garth, where Obie said they would be. You get them and head for the ranch. Or wherever you think it's best to go."

Tulley and Lenzie both stood erect, and Tulley said, "I'll sure come after you, Garth, and I won't stop till I get you. You have to take an oath to wear this badge."

"You won't lay a hand on him, Frank Tulley! I'll shoot you if you do."

Garth's knees gave way. He sank back down into the chair, weathered face contorted. "She will shoot, Frank," he said weakly.

"No, she won't. She knows I'm trying to help you folks, not hurt you. Effie, he's going back to jail whether I take him or not. If I don't do it, another sheriff will, because I'll be dead. Marshal Aikens will shoot me if I don't, and you're threatening to do it if I do. How many chances does that give me?"

He started toward her. Her eyes wavered. When he reached her, she became enraged at her own weakness and whirled away from him, crying out. Trying to take the gun away from her, he kept her from squeezing the trigger, but didn't realize how hard he gripped her wrist. Crying audibly, she surrendered the weapon, and Tulley let the hammer down, and that was all he knew. . . .

When he regained consciousness, he was lying on the rug, but his head was in a soft lap. He opened his eyes to stare into Katie's face as she bent over him. Her cheeks were wet with tears and she was still sobbing.

"What's the matter?"

His voice was a shock to her. She was silent for a moment and then began blubbering worse than ever. "I thought I had killed you."

He sat up, putting a hand to his head. Presently he said, "You've got yourself into a mess now. I can file half a dozen charges against you for what you did."

He got to his feet, took a step and staggered. He reeled to the sofa and slumped down. He put both hands to his head and groaned.

"What did you hit me with, Katie?"

"This," she said huskily.

He raised his head. She had picked up a shot-loaded quirt he hadn't noticed on the rug. She dropped the quirt and got to her feet, coming to stand before him. She searched his eyes and was thoroughly scared.

"I'm sorry," she said, sniffling.

"I don't blame you a bit, Katie."

He leaned back and passed a gaze around the

brightly lighted parlour, finding everything as it had been except that he and Katie were alone.

"I can stop them yet," he said, and sought to push himself erect. He fell back down, too weak and sick to stay on his feet. His six-gun was still in its holster, he realized, and he dozed off for a minute.

He felt Katie tugging at him. "Stretch out on the couch. Want some whisky?"

"No whisky."

Katie knelt on the rug, putting her face near his. "I heard what you said about Marshal Aikens, and I'm going to go see him, tell him it wasn't your fault. Tell him what I did, and if he wants to arrest me—"

Tulley groaned and sat up. "You never explain anything to a man like Aikens. It just makes matters worse. Besides, that would make me look like a simpleton—getting knocked senseless by a girl who won't weigh a hundred pounds wringing wet."

"Well—" she said helplessly.

"I'm getting all right now. But there's no hurry anyway. Garth can't get away from me. He's got too much at stake."

"You won't shoot him, will you?"

"Hell, no. Why should I? It wasn't him; it was his pants-wearing womenfolks."

Katie adjusted her skirt and seated herself beside him on the sofa.

"Why can't you just go up to the ranch and get Marie Simpson and have her tell Fred Blake what she saw at Jess Burk's place?"

"That was guesswork you overheard, Katie. Carnotte and Spaugh aren't legally guilty of that till a jury says so. Marie won't even tell me what she saw."

"She'll tell me," Katie said, pretty mouth twisting. "I'll scratch her eyes out if she says Daddy did that. I know he didn't. Vince didn't, either."

Frank Tulley said, "I may just forget about Garth, Katie. Horace Aikens has been wondering for a long time if he's faster with a gun than I am. This will give him a good excuse to find out."

"Frank, is it that bad?"

"It could be, Katie," Tulley said, and suddenly he cocked his head, listening.

"What is it?"

He motioned with a forefinger at Webb Colter's door.

"Webb's not there," Katie said. "He's down at his saloon, playing poker with some *hacendados* from over on the Clear Fork."

If Colter wasn't in his office, someone else was. Tulley had heard a man trying to repress an impulse to cough.

Katie said, "I never did hit anyone before."

"Just remember you don't have to strike a man as hard as you'd wallop a killer bronc."

"I won't ever strike a man again."

"I had it coming, scuffling with your mother that way. My mistake was in coming here like a friend instead of as an officer of the law. I should have pointed this Remington at Garth, told him he was under arrest and hustled him out. That's all there would have been to it."

Tulley leaned back with closed eyes, head aching, and considered his predicament.

Effie and Garth had headed for home by now, doubtless in the buckboard. Tulley could easily overtake them, but what good would that do? Jeffers and Sheppard and Potter were riding escort, and would use their carbines to halt pursuit. Shoot to kill, too.

No, Tulley wouldn't take out after Garth. He had to get the drop on Garth sometime when Garth was alone. Either that, or talk Garth into surrendering peaceably.

"I figure he'll head for Barrel Springs," Tulley said aloud.

"Who? Daddy? He won't head anywhere but home."

Tulley sat up straight. He looked down at Katie's hands. "When are you going to take that ring off, Katie?"

She dropped her gaze and covered her left hand with her right.

"Give it back to him," Tulley insisted.

"I can't."

"Well," Tulley said, "when I get Garth taken care of, you and I will talk it over, Katie. I don't believe you really love Webb Colter, and I don't want you to marry him."

Tulley had recovered sufficiently to move around. He got up and got his hat and put it on.

"What are you going to do now, Frank?"

"Follow Garth and Effie and Vince out to the G Bar L. You should have gone with them."

"I didn't want to go off and leave you lying on the floor, maybe dead. Please take me with you, Frank."

Tulley considered it. "I'd take you, Katie, but I'm afraid you'll trick me."

"Honestly, I won't. I've had time to think, and I realize we can't buck the law."

"All right. Go change your clothes. Can't fork a saddle in those fancy duds."

"Frank, I don't feel up to a horse. Let's get a buggy."

"Rent one?"

"No. You're the county sheriff. I'll bet there are a half-dozen buggies and buckboards in that county barn. Why can't we take one of them?"

"We can," Tulley said. "You really use your noggin, Katie. I'll go see what I can rustle up."

She followed him to the hall door and looked as if she expected him to kiss her.

Straightening his vest and gunbelt, he said, "Coming back here and finding you getting ready to marry someone else is pretty hard to take, Katie. Maybe it's the right thing to do. No matter how worthless a man is, he's generally considerate of his own woman if she'll let him be. You give Colter his chance."

"I will. Do you want me to stay here, or wait in the lobby, Frank? I'll leave the bags here."

"Wait for me in the lobby," Tulley said. He went out and slammed the door. Webb Colter was in his office, maybe, and would join Katie in the parlour now. Tulley would wait until he did and then have it out with the both of them. Katie Lenzie was Frank Tulley's girl.

Chapter Ten

At this late hour, although the saloons and cantinas were still open for business, Buffalo City had settled down for the night, the hitching rails empty and the sidewalks clear. It was quiet too, except for the stamping and squealing of broncs in the corral behind the stage station, and the usual smaller noises—owls hooting in the timber along the creek, dogs barking remotely, coyotes yapping. The night was perfect, Tulley thought; warm, and with a pale moon high in cloudless heavens. It was ideal for a long ride, and somewhere up there on that lonely trail to the G Bar L, Katie Lenzie would get sleepy, and in imagination, Frank Tulley could already feel his arms around her, her head on his chest, the remembered scent of her sachet at this instant vivid in his nostrils.

But he knew he was just taking everything for granted.

He didn't really know, for instance, that the three G Bar L hands had gone home with Garth and Effie. They might be yonder in the Parlour Saloon right now. Maybe he should go see, and if so, arrest Potter.

No, Garth Lenzie was the man in question. Garth was of first concern, and with him again behind bars, maybe Vince Potter would be easier to handle. Tulley didn't doubt for a minute that he would lock Garth Lenzie up eventually, if Marshal Aikens would give him time.

Proceeding toward the lighted windows of his office, Tulley passed through patches of moonlight and shadow cast by the trees on the square, and he halfway expected to find Horace Aikens' long body propped against one of those trees, waiting for him. But Aikens wasn't around.

In the adjoining block, Tulley could see that the windows of the marshal's office were lamplighted and his door was wide open, evidence that he hadn't wandered off very far. He could, therefore, be waiting for Tulley in the courthouse. Tulley wasn't afraid of Aikens, but he wasn't eager to fight him, either, if he had to fight him. And he *had* given Aikens his word about Garth Lenzie.

Letting himself into his office, Tulley headed for the rack of guns, not wanting to make a trip to the livery stable for his own weapon. He spent several minutes examining the rifles, and selected one just like his own, a sixteen-shot Henry.

Opening the breech of it then, he inserted a scrap of white paper that would reflect light up the barrel, and he squinted through the bore. The gun was cleaner than his own, he saw, and from the sharp look of the lands, he knew it was a newer gun. It would shoot true, and that's what he wanted. Close or far, he had to outshoot everyone now. Or he would find himself alongside Al Ramage over there in the mortician's in the rear of the furniture store.

Ramage had filled a desk drawer with assorted ammunition, and Tulley got a box of .44's, loading the rifle fully except for the firing chamber. Afterward, he searched for a lantern, pulling open the door of a closet. A brief glance showed him not only lanterns but boxes of candles and count-less other items needed by a county sheriff, including rain clothes for wet weather and canteens for dry.

There were handcuffs and leg irons and an Oregon boot, but Tulley wasn't interested in this paraphernalia. He certainly didn't intend to shackle any of the G Bar L men. He didn't aim to shackle anybody. If he couldn't handle a prisoner without putting cuffs on him, he'd buffalo him.

When he had one of the lanterns lighted, Tulley blew the office lamps out.

He locked the door behind him, wondering how long he would be gone. A trip to the G Bar L might take three or four days, depending on how tough it would be to bring in Garth and Vince.

Tulley's movements were considerably slower than they generally were, he realized. He hadn't had much sleep lately. The slug through the leg had given him trouble, and having been bashed on the head a while ago, he was far from being up to snuff. He'd hate to have to make a fast draw.

Tulley's spurs seemed to jingle unusually loud as he went along the corridor to the rear door.

Outside on the stoop he experienced again the peculiar feeling of being under the surveillance of someone who meant him evil. The hair on the nape of his neck stiffened.

Leaning the rifle against the doorjamb, he thumbed up the globe of the lantern and blew out the flame. The fact that he had lit the lantern before needing it was evidence that he wasn't thinking clearly, he told himself.

Carrying the rifle and lantern with his left hand, and keeping his right hand near the butt of his Remington, he glanced each way at the corners of the courthouse. He walked backward for a distance. The trees had been cleared off of this part of the square, but the stumps remained, leaving ample cover for a bushwhacker. No enemy lurked on this back side of the plaza, though.

The land sloped considerably to the street, which ran almost due north and south. Across the street were the county sheds and barn, looming huge in the moonlight. The gateposts were massive, and the gate itself wide enough for a hay frame.

Tulley freed his hands, reaching for the padlock, and let himself into the corral. When he had shut the gate, Tulley listened intently, sniffing the night air and catching the odour of street dust. A rider had been along the road recently, while Tulley was inside the courthouse, probably.

Wryly, Frank Tulley told himself that he was too jumpy. Maybe it was because of the lick on the head Katie had given him.

Moving on, he entered the barn, which had an open wagonway through the centre. On the right were doors which gave into rooms. Opening the first one, Tulley relit the lantern and held it high. Here were ropes and harness, packsaddles, stock saddles and other gear. Everything was orderly. The floor had been swept clean.

On the left side of the wagonway, beyond a row of posts which supported the hayloft and roof, were the county-owned vehicles, and Tulley noticed a red-wheeled buggy. Just the thing for him and Katie.

Earlier in the evening, Horace Aikens had recommended firing the handy man, Calico Thompson. He'd spoken of another fellow for the job of corral tender, but Tulley liked Thompson's work. There was no trash or litter or droppings in the barn whatever. Calico could keep the job.

Well, Katie was probably becoming impatient. Tulley would catch up a couple of broncs, slap harness on them, hook them to this red-wheeled buggy, and go get her. He moved out to the corral.

Frank Tulley never knew what warned him, but all at once he slung the lantern from him and hurled himself flat.

As the lantern described a high arc to crash against the corral fence, guns roared from the blackness of the barn. Tulley first thought he'd been shot in the face, but then he realized that a slug had showered him with a gout of dirt. He had his own gun drawn now.

He fired and rolled and fired again. He pushed onto his haunches and got his back to the outside of the harness-room wall.

Gunsmoke was acrid in his nostrils now and so was the stench of hot coal oil. The powder smoke haze of the barn was growing brighter. Tulley glanced around. Lurid flames near the corral gate told him that the spilled oil had caught fire.

The land sloped toward the barn. Unless the hard-packed ground soaked up the coal oil, the stuff would trickle downhill and set the barn afire; then everything this side of the street would go.

Frank Tulley held his breath.

He'd heard a rattling noise which seemed to be that of someone stumbling against a doubletree. The fire was lighting up the interior of the barn now, and Tulley saw the man, climbing into the wagon. Tulley waited.

A tongue of flame and smoke licked out at him from the bed of the wagon, and he pulled the trigger of his Remington.

The man in the wagon screamed, leaped upright

and tumbled onto a front wheel. He slid off the wheel onto the ground.

At this moment, another man emitted a hoarse bawl and broke and ran. He was silhouetted against the firelight, but Tulley didn't shoot him. It was Jules Carnotte. Outside the barn, he ran almost into the fire, seemingly close enough to singe his beard; then he whirled to head south. He took one step. Both his arms jerked upward spasmodically, and he pitched forward onto his face even as the roar of the gun out there lingered in Tulley's eardrums. Frank's first thought was that Marshal Aikens had joined in.

"Tulley?" the man near the wagon called weakly.

"What, Spaugh?"

"Nothing. Me and Jules killed Jess Burk, but Webb Colter didn't—" Tulley heard a gasp, a groan, and a strange utterance that told him Griff Spaugh was dead.

Getting to his feet, Frank sprinted as fast as his injured leg would permit, hoping to find Carnotte alive, wanting to hear more of what Spaugh had told.

Before Tulley was clear of the wagonway, however, he heard excited shouts. A group of men bore down upon the corral, the tall, stooped figure of Marshal Horace Aikens in the lead. Tulley had, therefore, been wrong. Someone else had killed Carnotte. Webb Colter, maybe?

Tulley wanted to catch him. Whirling about,

he trotted in the opposite direction and out of the barn at that end. Dimly, in the moonlight, he saw a man scrambling over the fence into the horse corral.

"Halt, or I'll shoot!"

The man didn't halt and Tulley didn't shoot. He couldn't be certain it was Webb Colter, either.

Running to the fence, Tulley jammed his Remington into its holster and went up and over, oblivious to his leg wound. His one purpose now was positive identification of Carnotte's killer.

In the horse pasture, Tulley ran in the direction taken by his quarry—straight toward the creek. Tulley lost sight of him in the brush. Because of the broncs in this corral, Tulley couldn't pursue him by the sound of his running.

Tulley splashed through the shallow creek, and then he heard the pounding hoofbeats. The man had reached his tethered horse, mounted it and was headed up through the timber.

Stopped abruptly by the fence, Tulley stood there a moment, debating. If one horse had been tethered out yonder, maybe two more were there—those of Spaugh and Carnotte.

Tulley easily located the two horses. He untied one of them, mounted up and rode in the direction taken by his quarry.

It was Webb Colter, undoubtedly, Tulley decided.

He pulled his borrowed horse to a jog trot and

then to a walk, telling himself that he was trying to make a manhunt out of it. What right did he have to do that, or even to think ill of the man he was pursuing?

He had forgotten all about the star on his vest.

If he ran that man down and cornered him and captured him, what would he charge him with? With being a hero? Buffalo City folks would commend anyone who joined in a gunfight on behalf of the county sheriff. With the body of Sheriff Al Ramage not yet cold, citizens hereabouts would feel like parading such a man around on their shoulders.

No use riding any further.

Reining the borrowed horse around, Tulley headed up out of the timber and for the plaza, intending to return to the barn.

The coal oil from the smashed lantern had burned itself out now, or had been put out by Aikens and the other men. Several lanterns were visible near the front of the barn, and in the smoke-scented air the talking was amazingly distinct.

One man said, "That's the way it generally happens. This town will be plumb peaceful for a spell; then all hell breaks loose, and half a dozen fellers will get plugged in a single night. Not always in the back, though," he added.

Frank Tulley reined up. He had to figure this thing out.

There were two dead men at the barn, and one

shot in the back. In all probability, Frank Tulley was the only one who knew there had been a fourth man there, that someone had fled after gunning down Carnotte from behind.

Tulley, himself, would be blamed with that. Sure, Aikens was there. Angry that Tulley had failed to keep his promise to bring in Garth and Vince, he would be delighted to accuse Tulley of back-shooting someone.

When you came right down to it, Tulley had no way of proving that he himself had been attacked. They might accuse him of jumping Jules and Griff. The pair had already filed one such complaint with Marshal Aikens, and Aikens would be ready to believe it now, unless he knew different. Everybody knew, or soon would know, that Tulley had had a quarrel going with that pair. Tulley had already heard someone quoting the conversation that had taken place in the cantina.

The fact that Tulley had first refused the sheriff's job could be held against him now. He had asked for the badge after quarrelling with Spaugh and Carnotte, and Aikens could say that Tulley wanted it only to hide behind it while tallying his enemies.

Tulley's head ached.

He wondered if Katie was still waiting for him at the hotel. He'd better go and see. She was more important right now than anything or anyone else.

He reined south, circling wide of the plaza, and passed behind Pemberton's wagon yard. He crossed the Double Mountain Road and approached the hotel from the rear. Before he dismounted at the foot of the outside flight of stairs, he tied the ends of the bridle reins together.

The borrowed horse immediately became interested in the mustangs in the stage company's corral, and moved over to thrust its nose through the fence. Tulley was through with it. Let Horace Aikens do something about that bronc, now that its owner was dead.

Some of the first floor windows in the hotel were lighted, and Tulley could see the kitchen help at work inside, mopping the floor. He climbed the outside stairs as quietly as he could. Reaching the landing, he stopped to reconnoitre the dimly lighted hall of the second floor before entering. He saw no one, and went along the hall to the main staircase, and descended to the lobby.

He saw no one here, either, except Walter, the clerk. Far from being drowsy, Walter was wide-eyed with excitement; he seemed almost bursting to talk, but restrained himself, an action that Tulley considered strange.

Tulley said, "You heard the shots and saw the fire, Walter?"

The clerk nodded, his Adam's apple jiggling as he swallowed.

"Couple of men—Jules Carnotte and Griff

Spaugh—waylaid me over at the county barn."

"Did they get away from you, Sheriff?"

"Both dead. Did anyone come in here recent? Lay it on the line, now, Walter."

"Mr. Colter did."

"That's not enough, Walter."

"Well, he was in a hurry. And mad. Katie Lenzie was over there on that sofa, and he said to her, 'If you're waiting for that tin-badge to take you home, you're going to be disappointed. He won't show up. He's off down yonder on the creek, sneaking around in the brush.' Miss Lenzie said, 'Those shots—what happened, Webb?' real scared-like. Mr. Colter said, 'I just killed a skunk,' and Katie cried out, 'Frank!' and that made Mr. Colter madder than ever. He said, 'Get yourself upstairs, you little wench, and stay there.' Miss Katie did, too."

"With Colter?"

"No, not with him. She lifted her skirts and ran up, and when she slammed her door it shook the hotel from stem to stern, almost."

Frank Tulley stood there a moment, enjoying the tableau pictured by the clerk. "Thanks, Walter."

"You're welcome. Enforcing the law is everyone's job, I always say, and this desk is a good place to learn what's going on. I've been behind it a long time, Frank, and I'll tell you one thing I've learned—it's best to take a stand. *Some* kind of a stand. Most men—and I mean real killers, too—like you better if you let them *know* you're against them. I believe they *respect* you for it!"

Tulley grinned. "May not be sound judgment, but it makes a man feel taller, eh, Walter?" He turned to the stairs.

Brows arched, the clerk nodded. "Can't get anywhere pussyfooting around."

Reaching the landing, Tulley pulled his Remington and reloaded it, and as he put the empty hulls into his pocket, he relived those seconds in the barn, hearing again Griff Spaugh's failing voice, and wondering what he had intended to say about Colter.

Well, Tulley told himself, he'd most likely never know.

Gaining the second floor, he turned toward the front of the building, but suddenly he changed his mind and stopped at one of Colter's doors, instead of Katie's. Out of deference to sleeping guests he drummed his knuckles quietly.

The summons brought Colter, but he didn't appear at the door Tulley had rapped on. He opened the centre door of his three-room suite. He stepped into sight in his shirt sleeves, shiny black hair neatly combed, moustached mouth clamped on a cigar. He was holding a newspaper and had moccasins on, Tulley noticed.

"Want to see me, Sheriff?"

"Uh-huh."

“Come in here, then. That’s my bedroom.”

Colter had undoubtedly shed his boots and coat and hat as well as his cartridge belt in his bedroom, and hadn’t stowed them out of sight.

Tulley was conscious of the mud on his own boots when he stepped onto the deep pile of Colter’s rug. A massive marble-topped table, long but narrow, stood near the windows. Twin lamps with painted porcelain shades cast a glow over a tray containing a decanter and several shot glasses. A box of cheroots lay there, too.

With an air of quiet dignity, Colter closed the door, turned his back and put the newspaper down on the sofa.

“Find the man you were looking for, Sheriff?”

“I think so.”

“Have a seat.”

Two armchairs, obviously built for big men and upholstered in red plush, were drawn up near the table, facing each other with a tall, polished spittoon beside each. Tulley took one, and was struck by the thought that the last man to share these chairs with Colter had been Horace Aikens. He didn’t say as much.

Colter turned to the table. Laying his cigar on the edge of the tray, he picked up the decanter.

“Like bourbon, Sheriff?”

“I don’t actually like it, Colter, but it would be a dreary world without it.”

“Isn’t that the truth?” Smiling faintly, Colter

filled two glasses. “Well, Tulley, I know your name and you know mine. I guess we’re acquainted, eh?”

“Both of us wanting the same girl,” Tulley said, “we’d better be acquainted.”

He accepted the glass of bourbon.

Switching his own glass to his left hand, Colter picked up his cigar, sank teeth into it, and sat down, saying, “I suppose you’re talking about Katie Lenzie. What makes you think I want her?”

“She thinks so. She’s proud of that ring.”

Colter took the cigar from his mouth and tasted the whisky. “Think you’ll like your new job?”

Tulley said, “If tonight’s a fair sample of it, I won’t.”

“It isn’t. You haven’t hardly had time to draw a long breath yet. It won’t all be ducking and dodging.”

“Some of it’ll be dancing in the streets, eh?”

“Scalp dancing?”

“Why, yeah. Anyhow that might be looked forward to.”

A sardonic gleam entered Colter’s dark eyes, and he asked, “Do you really intend to drink that whisky?”

Tulley lifted the glass so that lamplight shone through the liquor. “Looks like good stuff—right out of a charred keg,” he said.

“It is good stuff,” Colter said. He kept watching Tulley.

Tulley downed the drink and set the glass back on the tray. He said, "Smooth as silk, Webb, but whisky like that is wasted on me. I'm used to rotgut."

Colter had relaxed. His moustached mouth was smiling. "Do you want some rotgut?"

"No, thanks."

Colter lifted the box of cheroots off the table and held them toward his caller. Tulley took one. He stood erect to light it by holding the end of it above the chimney of one of the lamps. When he sat back down, he took off his hat and dropped it onto the rug and caught Colter eyeing the bullet hole in it, but the man didn't mention it.

Resting his arms on the red plush, Tulley said, "You give me the feeling that I've just passed inspection or something."

"You have. You never drink with a man you aim to kill, and you just had one with me."

"Talk gets around," Tulley said.

"Yes. Talk made by dangerous men."

Tone hardening, Tulley said, "Jules Carnotte and Griff Spaugh were called errand boys, or helpers, of yours. They tried to kill me. When they failed, did you shoot Carnotte in the back to cover up?"

"Nope. And they weren't errand boys or helpers; they just did chores for me occasionally."

"Like trying to kill Marie Simpson?"

"Of course not."

"They tried it."

"I'm not surprised. They've tried a lot of things." Colter put his glass down and tossed his cigar into the spittoon beside his chair.

"You sure hurried to get back here," Tulley said.

"Why, no. I never hurried. But where did you go?"

"I went up the creek a little way, trailing you," Tulley said. "Colter, I don't believe you came down to the barn to help me. It's just like I said—they failed, and you got even. And shut their mouths at the same time."

"Do you really want the truth, Sheriff?"

Tulley nodded.

"I sent Griff and Jules up to Jess Burk's place to rough him up a little because he wouldn't pay me for a team. That's all they did."

"Did you know about Marie Simpson? They scared her half to death and made her hurt herself. Did you tell them to do that? Lige Wessels was with them. What about him?"

"Lige wasn't supposed to be with them. I sent him across the creek on another errand."

"Lige killed Al Ramage, didn't he?"

Colter frowned. "How do I know? I was playing poker when that happened."

"Marie Simpson was an eyewitness to the Burk killing," Tulley said. "I think she told Ramage about it. He came straight back to town and turned Lenzie and Potter out of jail. Then he got killed. Why?"

"You're just guessing. Maybe it's coincidence. I think Garth Lenzie bought Ramage off. He was as crooked as a barrel of snakes."

"That's your opinion."

Colter's dark eyes narrowed. "Did you know Al Ramage?"

"No."

"Well, there was a lot of circumstantial evidence against Jules and Griff, their having been there at the Burk place, and chasing Marie to get the horse. With Garth Lenzie and Vince Potter free, Jules and Griff probably assumed that Ramage was going to throw them in. He could beat a confession out of a wooden Indian."

Tulley glanced at the smoke spiralling up from the cigar he held, and said nothing.

Quietly Webb Colter said, "I wouldn't knowingly let anyone harm a hair of Marie Simpson's head. I'm in love with that girl. She would be my wife at this very minute if she would have me."

"Bradshaw told me that Marie and Jess had been planning on getting married. Now I see why she was so terrified that night, Colter. She thought you had had Jess killed because of jealousy."

Colter nodded. "But I didn't have a thing to do with killing him."

Thoughtful, Tulley said, "What does Marie think about Katie wearing your engagement ring?"

"She understands it."

"But I don't," Tulley said.

Colter crossed his broadcloth-clad legs and tugged at a moccasin drawstring. "I gave that ring to Katie to keep down gossip. To protect her reputation. To show that my intentions were honourable."

"Maybe," Tulley scoffed. Presently he said, "You knew that Carnotte and Spaugh were going to waylay me at the barn. If you really did come down there to give me a hand, why did you do it? It wasn't on account of this star."

"I need you, Tulley. You used to be foreman of the G Bar L, and you know that ranch better than anyone. I want you to be foreman of it again, eventually."

"You're trying to get the G Bar L away from Garth Lenzie?"

Colter nodded.

"You won't."

"Well, that remains to be seen." Colter got up to pour more bourbon, his mouth, under the brush of dark moustache, set in hard lines.

Tulley stood up this time to accept the drink.

"To Katie's wedding," Colter said.

"I'll drink to that."

Setting the empty glass back on the tray, Tulley took a final drag on the cigar and dropped it into the spittoon. "I think you're just trying to throw me off guard. Either that, or you've learned that marrying Katie won't get you the ranch. You've learned that Effie will fight you both. She won't even will it to Katie if Katie is married toyou."

Colter stood there in his shirt sleeves, patiently determined to make Frank Tulley see things his way.

"Sheriff, I'm not trying to marry the G Bar L. I'm honest with you—I don't even want to marry Katie, lovely though she is. What could I do with a wife who held the purse strings? I know what being nagged means; my family taught me that. All I'm courting Katie for is to prevent bloodshed."

They were the same height, and Frank Tulley watched him levelly.

Colter said, "I don't want to spend any of my money hiring gun fighters."

"What do you mean?"

"I'm duty-bound to protect those farmers, and Garth would start a war of extermination on them if Katie would let him. Those clodhoppers can't fight, couldn't whip the G Bar L anyway. Not enough of them in the valley yet."

"That's what you aim to do—play up to Katie until you locate enough sodbusters here to take over the G Bar L?"

Colter sat down. "Can you think of a better way?"

"No," Tulley admitted. He sank back into his own chair, puzzled by Colter's frankness.

“But a man can’t make any real money off of nesters,” Colter said. “Might do it through politics, if this was a rich county, but it isn’t. I can make a little money by settling those hoemen on farms, but I’ll have to leave with it, or they’ll borrow it back from me. What I intend to do, Tulley, is bring in enough of them to get control of the G Bar L; then I’ll run every cussed one of them out of this valley.” Colter paused. “Or I’ll pay you to do it.”

Tulley gave him a sceptical grin. “How will you get control of Garth’s water holes? He won’t have to mortgage them to defend himself in court. He won’t ever come to trial for that Burk killing, because he didn’t do it, and too many people know that. You know it, yourself.”

Colter’s features became sardonic. “Innocent men have come to trial before, Sheriff. I’ll see to it that Garth gets in court. Besides, his water holes aren’t going to do him any good. If all the other land is taken up, he can’t run cattle on range that’s scattered section by section up and down the valley.”

Colter suddenly stood erect. “Sit still, Sheriff,” he said pleasantly. “I’ve got something I want to show you.”

Chapter Eleven

His moccasins soundless on the expensive rug, Webb Colter crossed the room and entered his office, closing the door behind him. Frank Tulley got up quickly then. He pulled his Remington and moved to a position to one side of the office door. Reappearing with a well-filled carpetbag, Colter jerked back, startled by the muzzle of Tulley's six-gun. Anger flared in his dark eyes, but he controlled it, and smiled.

"You had me worried there for a minute."

Tulley said, "That's the shape you had me in a while ago." Holstering his gun, he followed Webb Colter back to the two chairs.

Colter sat down and unlocked the bag and shoved it across the rug. "Take a look, Sheriff."

The carpetbag bulged with packs of beautifully lithographed certificates that were called Texas land scrip. Tulley dug down deep to make sure it wasn't just a four-flusher's bank roll—genuine certificates on top with stacks of paper cut to the same size underneath.

When Texas became the Lone Star State, Tulley knew, it retained ownership of its land, and issued these certificates, which called for a section each, in order to facilitate disposal of its public domain. They could be bought and sold or given away.

"Must be a million acres here," Tulley commented.

"Oh, no, not that much," Colter said. "But there's enough."

"You could sell them to that land company in Sherman for a fortune," Tulley said.

"But I don't intend to," Colter said. "I intend to acquire all of Garth Lenzie's open range with them. When I have the land above Double Mountain surveyed and recorded, I'll serve notice on him to stop running his cattle on it. And it will be your job to see that he does, Sheriff."

"Hope I'm not sheriff then."

Colter gestured persuasively. "I don't see why. You might as well share in it; someone will."

Tulley pushed the carpetbag back. "How did you find out that Garth's title was no good?"

"The same thing has happened in other countries. I read a newspaper account of the *Rancho de los Jaboncillos*, and then I started looking around for some other old grant that had been caught in the same squeeze. The G Bar L seemed to be my best bet. And here I am."

Locking the carpetbag, Colter got up to take it back into his office.

Setting his hat on, Tulley moved over near the hall door as Colter returned, his expression suave.

"I'm much obliged for the whisky and the cigar and the chin music, Webb. You sure have admitted being a top-hand skunk. Courting Katie and plan-ning to ruin that family. I'd like to shoot you right through the gizzard, but I can't. I can't even arrest you—yet."

Flushing, Colter said, "Arrest me? What for?"

Tulley's eyes slitted. "That's what I said—I haven't got any ground to arrest. I think the best thing for me to do is stomp hell out of you right here and now, Colter."

Colter's chin jerked up in alarm. He took a step backward, and landed against the sofa, as if to squat there. All at once he snatched up a derringer which the newspaper had been covering, the newspaper he had carried in his hand when answering Tulley's knock. Cocking the deadly little gun, he got up, advancing.

"Better take me seriously, Tulley."

"Why? You're just a dirty schemer. You're too big a coward to shoot me. You might not knock me out with one shot, and I'd have your neck wrung before you could shoot again."

Colter sneered, "Sure. You know I won't shoot you unless I really have to." Suddenly his left fist came up. The blow caught Frank Tulley on the cheekbone, staggering him.

He made it appear worse than it was. Reeling exaggeratedly, he managed to brush his hat against the wall and knock it off. He stooped as if to retrieve it. He came erect, right hand sweeping upward, fingers closing on the derringer. He drove his other fist into Colter's guts. Colter doubled forward and Tulley drove a knee against the man's jaw. Webb Colter had stamina. He stayed on his feet and recovered his breath even as Tulley stepped back with the derringer.

With the two-shot pistol pointed, Tulley moved around behind Colter and slapped his clothes for other hide-out weapons. Finding none, he shoved Colter toward the door of the bedroom.

"Get your boots on."

"What for?" Colter protested.

"I'm placing you under arrest. I couldn't do it a while ago, but I can now. You assaulted an officer of the law. That's a serious offence when I'm wearing the badge."

As he and Colter crossed the lobby, he heard the clerk in the alcove call, "Sheriff Tulley—?"

Both men stopped.

"Did Marshal Aikens find your room?" Walter asked.

"I didn't see him. Did he say what he wanted—leave any word?"

"No."

"Well, I'll probably run into him after a bit," Tulley said.

He and Colter went on.

"Horace might have come to my quarters, too," Colter said. "He may have heard us talking."

"If he did, he was mighty quiet about it."

"He can be quiet," Colter said. "Horace can sneak up on you like a redskin when he wants to."

They angled across the intersection to the plaza and were stopped by the sound of the horn which announced the approach of the stagecoach from Fort Griffin. They watched its running lights, heard the pop of the jehu's whip and listened to horse hoofs, harness and coach wheels.

"Horace is probably at the station now," Colter said. "He meets every coach to look over the new arrivals."

"Bounty hunting?"

"Perhaps. Or he may be hoping some noted gunman will hit town to match draws with him."

Tulley took Colter around to the rear entrance of the courthouse. Slamming and locking a cell door on the man, Tulley met his stare through the bars, as Colter said, "Frank, I should have known better than tackle you. You could whip a dozen like me without half trying."

"Yeah? I've met your kind before. A man like you can't be whipped. He has to be killed."

Abruptly Tulley turned away.

He went slowly along the corridor, a dull ache in his head from the blow Katie Lenzie had tendered him, feeling a twinge of soreness in his wounded leg with each step. He didn't want to stop going—there was so much to be done—but he had to rest. The one place in Buffalo City he could sleep without being disturbed would be his office. If someone tried to break in on him there, he could shoot to kill, knowing he wasn't shooting some drunk who'd made an error in a hotel room.

He let himself into the office and made his way across the room without lighting a lamp. Almost to the door of the room containing the bunks, he suddenly halted, not even breathing as he listened. He had heard a gun hammer go to full cock.

Calico Thompson's voice came then. "Who is that?"

"Who else has keys to this office, Calico, except you and me?"

"Nobody. But some folks don't need a key to get through a locked door, son. I'm plumb boogered, I reckon. It was you not lighting a lamp that scared me. Don't you want no light?"

"No."

Tulley went on into the bunkroom. The oldster's voice had indicated which bunk was unoccupied, and Tulley took off his gunbelt. Sitting down afterward to pull off his boots, he said, "Why aren't you up at the livery stable?"

"Well, all that excitement down at the barn brought Dave Hildebrand out, and I made him take over. You got Griff and Jules, eh? Say, son, that there horse that Wessels rented came back."

"Any blood on the saddle?"

"Not a speck."

"Then Wessels is probably headed for Fort Griffin."

Tulley undressed and straightened out on the bunk.

Calico Thompson said, "I was right glad to hear you was sheriff, Tulley. It's like Obie Sheppard said—I've been Al Ramage's right-hand man. If you ain't got nobody else in mind, I'd sure like to keep on the way I've been doing, taking care of the livestock and suchlike. I was waiting here to ask you about it, and dozed off."

"I'll study about it."

"Want me to leave now? So you can sleep? Want me to turn in these keys?"

"Calico," Tulley said, "it seems to me you knew a lot about Al Ramage's business, the danger he was in. Why didn't you tell him about it?"

"I did. I warned him. I told him he was liable to get shot and I named the man who'd shoot him. Al just laughed at me."

"Mind repeating that name?" Tulley asked.

"Damned right I mind. Find out for yourself."

Tulley was thoughtfully silent. After a bit, he said, "You can keep your job, Calico, till something better turns up."

"Something better? Ain't nothing better going to turn up for me, son. Before you go to sleep, I wish you'd give me some instructions about what time you want to be rousted out."

"Don't roust me out. Let me sleep. When you leave, lock the door, and don't tell anyone I'm here. Go up to the livery stable and get my saddle, Calico. And bring that G Bar L horse down to the county corral."

"That all?"

"My carbine. Did you take care of it?"

"Yeah," Calico Thompson said, and pretty soon Frank Tulley was snoring.

It was mid-afternoon when Tulley awakened. Calico was gone. He had made his bunk up neatly, and seemed to have left no sign of having been in the room, or in the office.

The courthouse was strangely silent. Tulley had figured that a county courthouse was a busy, noisy place. The town itself was quiet. The office windows had been lowered a foot or so at the top, and the usual noises of this town, always rowdy ones, should have been audible. Puzzled, not yet thoroughly awake, Tulley took a look out the windows.

There was no one on the plaza, no wagons or rigs on the streets, either. A few loungers were in sight on the store-porch benches, but not nearly as many as there should have been on a sunny afternoon.

What about Webb Colter?

Tulley got ready to leave the office and went down the corridor. A glance showed him that

Colter was gone. Marshal Aikens had turned him loose, of course. Still, Aikens wasn't the only one carrying keys to these cells. Calico Thompson had a set.

Horace Aikens had refused to take the sheriff job. Hadn't wanted it because the merchants paid him more money for keeping the town tamed with his gun. Now Tulley really understood what Aikens had meant when he claimed that the sheriff's job would take him away from Buffalo City too much. Aikens had to be here because he was not only drawing marshal's pay, he was probably also serving as Webb Colter's body-guard. Or so it seemed. *Lucky I didn't stop a slug last night,* Tulley thought grimly.

Tulley walked on down to the corral then, and he knew now where everyone was—at Boot Hill, of course, attending Al Ramage's burial service. And Carnotte's and Spaugh's, too, no doubt.

Even though it had looked that way last night, bright sunlight revealed that the barn hadn't been in the least danger of catching fire. There was a sizeable patch of blackened ground inside the corral, but quite a distance away from anything combustible.

The taxpayers could thank old Calico Thompson for that, because he had kept the straw raked up and forked into a pile in a fence corner.

From this lower elevation Tulley couldn't see much of the town, but he could hear an anvil ringing, which meant that George Bankston, or a hired hand, hadn't cared much for Al Ramage, not knocking off work to attend the funeral. Down the creek, saw-and-axe noise indicated that the local wood choppers hadn't, either.

The rifle Tulley had dropped here was gone, taken care of by Calico Thompson, probably. Tulley went over then to stare at the wagon Griff Spaugh had tumbled out of, mortally wounded. What else had Spaugh been intending to say about Webb Colter?

Well, with the man dead, Tulley could only guess now.

Panic had flushed Jules Carnotte out, Tulley saw when he went over to the corner where Jules had lain in wait for him. Jules had been forted up behind a slip used for road building, and not even the Henry rifle would have driven a bullet through the piece of grading machinery. "It was just his time to say amen," Tulley muttered.

Everything was in good order in the harness room. Tulley's saddle was swinging by the horn from a loop of rawhide, evidence that Calico Thompson had followed orders. There were other saddles in the room and ropes, too, but Tulley took his own lariat and went down to rope a mount.

He saw the broncs that Ramage had brought Garth Lenzie and Vince Potter to town on, but he couldn't find the one that he, himself, had ridden in from the G Bar L, the one he had told Calico to bring down here.

Maybe Cleon or Obie had led the horse back to the ranch.

If so, they had no right to, considering that Tulley's private horse was still at the G Bar L. Telling himself that maybe he had overlooked the horse in the brush, Tulley caught up a big grey.

When he left the corrals, he rode up the creek to a water hole deep enough to swim in. When he returned to the courthouse, he noticed that the mourners had come back to town now.

Tying up back of the building, Tulley went along the corridor and suddenly stopped, hearing angry voices. One was Calico Thompson's. Two other men were with Calico, arguing, gesticulating. His attention caught by the sound of Tulley's spurs, Calico whirled around, fairly bristling.

The cause of the argument was on the floor. Tulley saw a box of tools, a spigot, an unopened packing box and a cradle on which lay a twenty-gallon keg.

"Sheriff Tulley, they're trying to say you ordered this keg of spirits!"

They were burly, unshaven men whose clothes and laced boots were like the garb worn by teamsters.

Tulley said, "Open up for them, Calico."

"What?"

"I didn't order it, but we'll take it."

Reluctantly Calico Thompson fished out the key. "Well, it's your business, not mine, Sheriff, but I'll venture to say you won't go very far or last very long, drinking on the job."

Tulley said, "It's according to who you're drinking with and why, Calico," and he watched the oldster swing the door open. Indignantly Calico stalked out then.

Tulley took the swivel chair at his desk and looked on while the men tapped the keg, drove in the spigot and opened the packing box, which contained tin cups. When they had finished, Tulley said, "Help yourself, fellows."

Neither accepted the invitation. They left hastily, gingerly.

Tulley followed them as far as the courthouse steps, and saw them climb into a delivery hack drawn by a team of Percherons. It was Ben Mullins' hack.

Calico Thompson had stopped on the steps, even-tempered again.

"If Ben sent that over from the Parlour, he must have had a keg of it in stock," Tulley thought aloud.

"What's that?" Calico asked.

"I was just talking about that whisky."

Calico said, "I got your gun and saddle, son. Your horse wasn't there. The Lenzie girl forked it about daylight this morning and never came back. I came by the hotel and she hadn't showed up there since breakfast. I went upstairs and their stuff was all in their rooms, but Katie wasn't. I reckon she struck out for home."

"Was Colter there?" Tulley asked.

"No, he wasn't. But his doors wasn't locked. He wouldn't head off up to the G Bar L, if that's what you're thinking, and leave his office unlocked. Katie went by herself."

"Did you turn Colter out of the lockup, Calico?"

The oldster looked up at Tulley vaguely.

"I put him in jail early this morning, and he was gone when I went back to see about him. I thought maybe you opened up for him."

"No."

"Better stay away from Colter's office, Calico. I wouldn't be prowling around it when he's not there."

"Pshaw—Webb don't pay me no mind."

Tulley went down the courthouse steps then, leaving the oldster perplexed and worried. Calico watched him until Tulley reached the hotel.

The lobby was quite crowded and everyonc was dressed in his finery, because of the burial services.

Tulley was famished. It was too early for supper, but he hadn't yet had breakfast and dinner. He went on back to the dining room, which was open at all hours but served only lunches at this hour.

John Pemberton was there, and Tulley went

over and sat down by him. Pemberton had turned considerably greyer in the last five years, and had lost more hair from the top of his head. And more teeth from his jaws, too, judging from his sunken cheeks.

"Frank," the storekeeper said, "you'd better let the situation cool off a little. You're taking your job too seriously."

"I didn't kill both of those men, John. Webb Colter shot one of them."

"Yes, I know. Fred Blake told me."

Tulley gave the serving girl an order for coffee, ham and eggs, and then asked the storekeeper, "How'll I go about letting it cool off, John?"

"Well," Pemberton said, nursing his coffee cup, "three killings took place last night. Take that on top of what happened to Jess Burk, and it makes for a bad state of affairs. It wouldn't take much more to stampede those hoemen, and no telling what might happen then. They might descend on this town and hang every public official here."

"You're talking wild, John."

"It has been done."

Ben Mullins entered the dining room from the pantry. He took a chair across from Tulley.

Pemberton said then, "Ben, what do you think about sending the sheriff out of town for a few days? We want him to keep wearing that star, not get himself killed like Al did."

"Good idea," Mullins wheezed. "You're running things, John, as far as I'm concerned." Lifting his fat-crowded eyes to the girl who was serving Tulley's ham and eggs, he asked her to bring him some custard pie and milk.

"Why do you think the nesters might take their spite out on the county officials, John?"

"Up to now, Frank, working for Webb Colter, Griff and Jules—and Lige Wessels, too—have been thick as thieves with the grangers. They've been lollygagging some of their womenfolks. With the county sheriff getting credit for killing them, it put those hoemen in a bad mood."

"The hoemen got double-crossed," Tulley said.

"Well," the storekeeper said, "let it ride for a while. Forget about Garth Lenzie, too. In the morning I'll provide you with a list of delinquent taxes, and you can see what can be done with it. A list that'll take you west of the Yeguas."

"All right."

Mullins wheezed, "Dunning the nesters for their taxes the first crack out of the box won't look good for Frank. It won't help him get elected, come November."

"That won't matter," Tulley said. "If they owe it, I'll ask them for it."

They finished their food and coffee and milk in silence.

"Have you seen Colter today?" Mullins asked Tulley.

"No."

"He's sure in a foul mood. He came over there to the Parlour to borrow a keg of bourbon from me, and he was all puffed up."

"Maybe because I tossed him in jail," Tulley said.

John Pemberton shook his head. "That wasn't it. He told me about that and didn't seem sore."

"Did he tell you what the trouble was?"

"Said you all had a quarrel over Katie Lenzie and that he lost his head and struck you."

"Well," Tulley said, "that's as good an explanation as I could give." He pulled out the money to pay for his meal.

Pemberton said, "Never mind. I'll take care of it, Frank."

"It's all on the house," Mullins wheezed, and Tulley took leave of them.

Coming through the crowded hotel lobby that night, Tulley passed his gaze over several people gathered at the desk, and he suddenly stopped. One of the newcomers was Gil Jebb, Garth Lenzie's foreman. What was Jebb doing in town? Moving over to a leather couch, Tulley sat down to wait, intending to have a talk with Jeb.

Behind the desk, glistening in the slanting light of the chandelier, Walter's pomaded head kept bobbing at the others ranging before him, and Gil

Jebb impatiently turned away to pace across the room.

Tulley stood up. “In a hurry, Gil?”

The squint-eyed man appeared startled; then his expression became guarded. He had just come from the barbershop, apparently. Letting his glance rest briefly on Tulley’s star, he shook his head.

“Why should I be?”

“Didn’t you come to get the Lenzies’ belongings?”

“No. I’m not interested in the Lenzies’ belongings.”

“What do you mean, Gil?”

“I quit.”

Tulley indicated the couch. “Sit down, and let’s talk it over. Who’s taking your place?”

“Obie Sheppard.”

Tulley considered it. “What happened between you and Garth?”

“We just don’t see eye to eye, that’s all. I hired out to him to be foreman of a cattle ranch. What he wants now is a *segundo* who savvies gun fighting, and I don’t. I won’t ride at the head of an outfit of gunmen.”

“That sounds kind of funny, coming from you, Gil. When you and Tom and I got into it over Marie Simpson, a gun was the first thing you grabbed.”

Jebb frowned. “That was different. Tom Bradshaw was going too far—trying to keep an officer of the law from questioning someone. I'll draw my gun any time on the side of the law. You're sheriff now. That's all right with me. I'll give you a hand any way I can. Except I won't be around long."

"Where are you going, Gil?"

"Wherever the trail leads. I was on the go when I landed here. And I haven't done too bad in this valley, up to now."

"Well," Tulley said after long thought, "you can do even better here if you want to."

"What are you talking about?"

"How would you like to be my deputy?"

Gil Jebb stared. "You don't mean it."

Tulley fished the badge out of his pocket. "Try me and see."

Jebb hunched down on the couch, contemplating the risks of the proposition.

Tulley said, "I'm just finishing out Al Ramage's term. I won't toss my hat into the ring next election. You can serve as my deputy, and if you like badge-packing, you can run for sheriff yourself. Ever had any experience behind a badge?"

"No."

"Well, I haven't, either. I'm going to be gone for three or four days, collecting taxes, and I'll start beating the bushes for you right now. I'll do all I can to help you win."

Gil Jebb sat up straight and moved his gaze over the crowded lobby, as though picturing himself strolling through here with a law badge on his chest. All at once, needled by suspicion, he turned to Tulley and asked, "Got some particular chore in mind?"

"You mean something I'm afraid to do myself?"

"That's right."

Tulley shook his head. "Not something I'm scared to do. But I do have a particular job for you. Someone has to ride the stagecoach to Fort Griffin and bring back the man suspected of killing Al Ramage."

Without hesitation, Gil Jebb said, "Sure. I'll do that."

Tulley said, "Without even asking who he is? How dangerous he is?"

"If he has to be arrested, it doesn't make much difference, does it?"

"Not a bit. It's Lige Wessels, and he'll back down when he knows he's cornered. We'll find out from Fred Blake, the county attorney, what the procedure will be. But make no mistake about it, Gil—I want Lige placed under arrest and brought back, not shot. I'm none too sure he's guilty of killing Ramage."

"I wouldn't shoot anyone except in self-defence."

"You may have to now, Gil. An officer of the law has to shoot in defence of other people, too."

"Yeah, that's right."

Tulley stood erect. "Let's go," he said.

Chapter Twelve

Early the following morning, Deputy Sheriff Gil Jebb left for Fort Griffin armed with a warrant, and in less than an hour after the stagecoach had rattled away from the station, Frank Tulley left the hotel dining room, where he had eaten breakfast with the three county commissioners, and walked down to the corrals.

A few minutes later, Tulley rode back to the rear stairway of the hotel and loaded his saddle with a carbine, bedroll and a bulging pair of *alforjas*.

He, too, left Buffalo City then, heading first for a sodbuster layout away over near the county's north-west line.

Tulley was well beyond the boundary line of the old Contreras Grant here, and these farmers were old settlers. Delivering the tax notices, Tulley mostly talked politics and recommended Gil Jebb as successor to Al Ramage. He didn't receive much encouragement in this respect, but most of the grangers forked over the tax money. Complying with instructions from the county commissioners, Tulley was back in Buffalo City on the fourth day.

It was around nine o'clock in the morning when he rode down to the corrals. Calico Thompson was there and took care of his horse. Leaving some of his belongings in the harness room, Tulley roped and saddled a fresh mount and rode up to the hotel.

He entered his hotel room to stand amazed. During his absence, the room had been thoroughly ransacked. It took him several moments to grasp the situation. Even then he couldn't imagine what anyone would be searching for here in his quarters. He had filled it with clothes and other necessities needed for meagre living, but he had stashed nothing of value here.

And nothing had been taken.

Still thinking on it, Tulley shaved and washed up and donned clean clothes. He went downstairs for pie and coffee afterward, and rode back to the courthouse. He tied up behind the building.

He stopped only briefly in his office, where Calico Thompson had just begun the chore of cleaning the guns in the wall rack.

"Who was messing around my room?" Tulley demanded.

"Wasn't me, son."

"I wasn't accusing you. I thought maybe you might know something about it."

"Well, it's like I told you down at the corrals, son; Webb Colter is madder than a teased snake. Maybe he was. Seems to me like somebody said they saw him coming out of your room, but I can't recollect now who it was."

"Well, I'm madder than a teased snake, myself."

"You throwed Webb in jail, didn't you?"

Tulley gestured impatiently. "It wasn't that. He was looking for something."

"You've been talking about trail driving and such-like. Webb might not have been the one who tore up your room. Somebody might have been looking for a cache of dinero."

"I don't think so," Tulley said.

He went out into the corridor, heading for the flight of stairs in the centre of the building. On the second floor, he left the tax money with the county clerk, and when he emerged from that office, he met Fred Blake, the county attorney. Blake had Webb Colter in tow.

Colter grunted a dour greeting.

The attorney was a hard-jawed big man, conservatively attired, with a shock of wavy brown hair. His eyes were a darker brown, and contained a certain cautious doggedness. Stabbing a finger at Frank Tulley, he said, "Why don't you stay in your office, Sheriff?"

"Am I supposed to?"

"You ought to be there when I need you," Blake said. He motioned for Tulley to come along. With the tramp of their booted feet echoing hollowly on the board floor, the three of them entered Blake's office.

Frank Tulley was taken aback then, by the sight of three people seated in chairs ranging around the prosecutor's desk: Marie Simpson and her father and mother.

There was no exchange of greetings, just covert glances.

Marie's big-shouldered blond father was wearing the same baggy suit of store clothes he'd had on the last time Tulley had seen him. That was the day he and Al Ramage had come to the G Bar L. Right now Mose had an unhealthy pallor. He was scared stiff, Tulley decided.

Marie and her mother were attired in crisply starched dresses, which meant that the Simpsons hadn't just completed a trip down a dusty road. They had probably been in town overnight and had stayed with friends.

Marie's bright yellow hair was lovelier than ever even though her dainty face was masklike. She kept her gaze on Fred Blake after one furtive glance at Tulley.

Blake moved around behind his flat desk and picked up a paper. He said to Tulley and Colter, "Mose and Maudie and Marie stayed with us last night, and I've already heard what she is going to tell. Before it goes any further, I wanted you men to hear it, and then advise me what to do."

Webb Colter said surlily, "Get on with it, Fred."

Blake sat down and fixed his attention on the girl. "You visited Jess Burk and he took your horse down to his barn and unsaddled it—"

"Wasn't Jess that unsaddled it. It was my daughter. And it wasn't her horse. It was Jess's."

"It was my horse," Colter said.

"All right," Blake said. "Now, Marie. You and Jess walked back across the road, and he was carrying your single-shot Sharps carbine. You saw two men coming along that road from the direction of town. Jess handed your gun back. He told you to go back to the barn and hide. He said there might be trouble."

Marie nodded.

"What happened then?" Blake prompted.

Marie tossed her head and smoothed her hair and audibly swallowed. "I went down to the barn, and Jess went into the house. The men stopped their horses in the yard. One of them yelled at Jess to come out, because he knew Jess was there. Jess came out onto the porch and stopped."

"He wasn't armed?" Blake suggested.

"No."

Blake said, "Go on."

"One of the men cursed. He yelled, 'I said come here.' Jess went down into the yard. He went to that man, and the other man reined his horse around and hit Jess with his pistol-l-l—" Sobbing, she put her head down.

Dark eyes inscrutable, Webb Colter moved up behind and leaned forward to say, "Crying won't do you a bit of good."

Marie straightened in the chair, and Blake said,

"After the man hit Jess with the pistol, what happened?"

Marie's voice was choked with tears. "They both got off of their horses. One of them kicked Jess and stomped him. The other man took out a long knife and—" She couldn't continue, and sat there reliving the experience, lips quivering.

Webb Colter said, "We came here to hear your story, Marie. What's the rest of it?"

Marie pulled a handkerchief from her sleeve to blow her nose. "Well, I had my Sharps, and I tried to shoot those men, but my gun wasn't loaded."

"Should it have been?" Blake asked.

"Yes. I loaded it before I left home. Jess must have taken the shell out of it."

"Levered it out accidentally," Blake suggested.

"You have to take your fingers and pull them out."

Blake nodded.

"I had three shells in my pocket and got them out, but I dropped them. I was crying, I guess, now, and couldn't see, couldn't find the shells in the straw. Soon enough, I mean. I did find them. Those men had dragged Jess into the house, though, and set the house on fire. It was kind of dark in the barn. I heard one of the men coming toward the door. The other man said, 'Touch off that pile of hay there by the wall. That will do it. Let's get gone.' I ran back and put the bridle on my horse and rode out of the barn. The men had headed toward Double Mountain—"

"Toward town," Blake said.

"No. I shot at them and they spurred off into the woods."

Webb Colter said, "You haven't named those men yet, Marie. Your purpose in coming here was to identify those killers, wasn't it?"

"Yes," Marie said, and was silent.

Mose Simpson said, "Them men was Garth Lenzie and Vince Potter." He looked at his wife. "Wasn't it them, Maudie?"

Mrs. Simpson's pinched features formed a grimace, but she nodded and said, "Yes, sir, it was them."

"Mose," the attorney said slowly, "you and Maudie didn't witness that crime. You may be repeating what Marie told you, but she'll have to speak for herself now."

Marie remained silent, her delicate features stony.

Webb Colter bent over and whispered to her. She turned her face to him and whispered back. He asked aloud, "After I'm dead?"

Fred Blake said, "Webb, you're coaching her."

"I have a right to. I'm her lawyer."

Marie faced the prosecutor again. "Yes, sir, that's who it was—Garth Lenzie and Vince Potter."

Uneasily, Blake stirred in his chair. He flicked

a glance at Tulley. He ran a finger around his collar. "What happened after they rode off into the timber, Marie?"

"I followed them. They got away from me. They never did come back to the road. Then I met three other men, and they wanted my horse. I didn't want to walk, so I made my horse run and got away from them. They chased me all day. They shot at me. At first, two of them didn't want to do that, but the other man told them to."

"Who was he?" Blake asked.

"Lige Wessels."

"And the other two men?"

"Griff Spaugh and Jules Carnotte."

"Why would Wessels want to shoot at you when the other two didn't?"

Mose Simpson, anticipating Marie's reply, said, "My daughter is a respectable girl, sir, no matter what they say about her."

"Go ahead, Marie."

"The man with the beard yelled, 'Don't shoot at her. She's Webb Colter's woman.' And then the little man laughed. He said, 'If she's Webb's, what was she doing in Jess Burk's barn?' "

Blake held up a restraining hand. "You're talking about different men now. How did these men know you were in Jess Burk's barn?"

Marie bit her lip. "Wessels had been there before, at Jess's place. He'd seen me there."

"All this time Jess Burk's place was burning," Blake said.

"But we were miles away. Away up past the G Bar L ranch."

Blake shifted uneasily in his chair. "Carnotte and Spaugh are dead, and Lige Wessels is a fugitive. Can't be questioned. What happened next, Marie?"

"Wessels said if you fellows were ordered to bring back that horse, that they had better get it. The red-headed man hollered at him, 'Don't try to take charge, Lige. You ain't giving us orders, and Webb Colter ain't, either.' "

Marie paused.

Blake said, "You finally got away from them."

"When it commenced storming, I did. My horse got struck by a bullet, or frightened some way, and stampeded. I lost my rifle. The next thing I knew, Sheriff Tulley was with me. Only he wasn't sheriff then." She shrugged. "He knows the rest of it better than I do."

The prosecutor swung his gaze to Tulley. "What's your verdict, Frank?"

"I'm not prepared to say right now, Fred. It looks to me, though, like Colter, there, set a hen and somebody robbed the nest. I believe, too, that these people—Mose and Maudie and Marie—are in grave danger. Marie will have to be available, of course, but I suggest we send Mrs. Simpson, and Mose, too, if he'll go, somewhere to a place of safety until we get this thing settled."

Blake nodded, lowered his gaze and continued to write for a time. He said finally, "Marie, you can sign this statement. And you and Frank can sign it as witnesses, Webb."

The three of them affixed their signatures.

"Carnotte and Spaugh and Wessels were working for me," Colter said. "I did send Carnotte and Spaugh up there after the horse Marie was riding. But that's as far as I'm implicated."

The attorney said, "It'll all come out in court, Webb." Blake then stood up behind the desk and took out a roll of banknotes. "I'm going to take the sheriff's advice. Maybe you folks are in danger and maybe you're not, but I'm going to send you and Maudie to San Antonio for a while, Mose." He tossed some money onto the desk. "You'll need that. I'll charge it up to the county somehow. When you get there, be sure and call for your mail regularly so we can keep in touch with you."

"What about our little girl?" Simpson cried.

Fred Blake's expression became official. "I can't tell you that. It's according to what she says when the court puts her under oath." He looked at the sheriff. "Will you see to it that Mose and Maudie are on the next eastbound stage?"

"Sure I will, Fred."

Mose Simpson asked, "Who'll look after our place? Who'll feed and water our horses and cows and chickens?"

"I'll send a man up there to do it," Blake told him.

Simpson gave his head an uncertain jerk. "I just don't know—"

Tulley said, "You want to live, don't you, Mose?"

Simpson picked up the money with alacrity and stepped back beside his wife.

Tulley turned to the attorney. "What about Marie?"

"She'll do all right with me and my wife," Blake said. "I wouldn't let you lock her up." Thoughtfully he tapped Marie Simpson's deposition. "This calls for the arrest of Garth Lenzie and Vince Potter, Frank."

"I know. I'll go up there and get them. But I'd like to take that paper along if you don't mind."

"No," Blake said, "I don't mind. But I hope you get back with it. And two prisoners."

Frank Tulley installed Mose and Maudie in a hotel room and ordered them to stay there until he returned for them.

A little later he walked into his office. Webb Colter was there, standing near the whisky keg. Calico Thompson was there, also, but he drifted out.

"Say, Webb," Tulley asked, "did you find what you were looking for?"

"What do you mean?"

"While I was out of town on those tax matters,

someone ransacked my hotel room. I think it was you."

Colter's gaze shifted.

"Went off half-cocked, didn't you, Webb? You didn't think. Just acted. You just rushed in and tore my room upside down. Don't tell me I was the only thief you could name offhand."

"Who should I have named?"

"Well, Katie Lenzie, maybe."

Colter shook his head. "Not her. She thinks they're counterfeit."

Frank Tulley sobered. "Webb," he said, "you really are a skunk. You told Katie those land certificates were bogus, and you've had her fighting her own father, thinking you didn't really mean Garth any harm. Katie thought you were helping him, that you were building a fire under him so that he would hustle around and get title to his rangeland."

Colter moved restively. He gestured at the keg. "How's the bourbon?"

"I haven't sampled it yet."

"Better hoist one, hadn't we?"

Tulley studied him a moment, and then said, "Sure, I'll drink with you. I'll drink with you, Webb, but I won't fight for you. You'll have to do your own."

Chapter Thirteen

It was sundown before Frank Tulley got ready to head for the G Bar L. While he saddled up, Calico Thompson caught up the two G Bar L mounts in the back corral for him. Leading the broncs, Tulley rode up to the rear of the hotel and went upstairs to get Tom Bradshaw's hat, which he carefully stowed in a saddlebag.

While he was fastening the saddlebag buckle, Marshal Aikens emerged from the rear door of the stage station and climbed over the corral fence to join him.

"Fred Blake told me about Marie Simpson's statement. Said he had an airtight case against the G Bar L now. You're holding her, eh? Where is she—want me to keep an eye on her while you're gone?"

"No. She'll be all right."

A faint smile touching his narrow, sideburned face, Aikens stood on spread heels, the fingers of his right hand gripping the edge of his long, square-cut black coat. His thick-lidded eyes were sceptical.

"That statement she gave Fred isn't worth a damn. I'll bet you my hat against yours that she doesn't know Garth Lenzie. She's never been right up close to him. Put him among a dozen others, all dressed alike and all of them about his age, and she'll be cornered."

"That's what we want," Tulley said. "That'll clear Garth."

"But hold on. Webb Colter doesn't want it. When he finds out that Marie can't identify Garth, he'll kill her."

"How would that help him, Horace?"

"It would make her written statement as good as gold. With her dead—mysteriously killed—that paper would put a rope around Garth Lenzie's windpipe."

Tulley shook his head. "Webb Colter wouldn't go that far, Horace, even to win the G Bar L."

"He's already gone that far. Griff and Jules were working for him. Didn't they try to kill Marie up there on the G Bar L range?"

"Yeah."

"If I were you, Frank," Aikens said seriously, "I wouldn't leave town without taking that girl with me. That is, if you want her to live. I'll tell you what would really be best for all concerned—empty your six-shooter into Webb Colter's guts. Somebody will have to do it, sooner or later."

"I'll let you do it, Horace."

"He's quit wearing his gun."

Tulley said nothing further. As he swung into the saddle, Aikens asked, "Can you bring Garth in all by yourself?"

"I don't know," Tulley said. He meant it.

He went up the Double Mountain road, lifting his horse to a hand-gallop, and the led horses raised dust behind him.

The air was sultry where the nesters' cornfields had sponged up the day-long sunshine, and the undersides of Tulley's Levi-clad legs were soon wet with sweat.

Fred Blake had found a hired hand to send up to the Simpson place, but the fellow wasn't going to work until tomorrow, and Tulley had promised to stop there.

He reached the Simpson place after dark, unsaddled his mount and turned all three horses into Simpson's barnyard. He forked down hay and pumped the trough full of water. Mose kept bran on hand for his cows. Tulley measured out feed for them and then turned the calves in with them, not being a very good milker. The cow pasture enclosed part of the branch for water.

Divesting himself of dust and sweat, Tulley headed for the smokehouse finally. Mose had plenty of meat. There was plenty of butter and eggs and other grub, too, Tulley discovered, and after he had eaten, he bedded down for a few hours of sleep.

He took care of the livestock again before daylight, and rode on toward the G Bar L.

Far beyond Double Mountain he heard the horse bells tinkling in the hazy dawn ahead, and he now turned Lenzie's led horses loose, so that they could join the remuda.

When the night wrangler took the remuda in, Tulley rode in behind it. The remuda swerved off toward the corral, hoofs pounding, bells clanking and dogs yelping like all get-out. Frank Tulley angled straight on and ascended to the tree-studded eminence on which the ranch house sat.

The front door was open with a lamp still burning in the hallway, and Tulley dismounted at the front gallery and tethered his horse. He went up the steps and saw Garth coming along the hall.

Garth barred his way with a six-shooter. Grizzled mane of hair standing on end, the rancher said, "If you aim to visit us, Frank Tulley, go back to your horse and shed your gun-belt and star!"

"You don't really mean that."

"Take that blamed star off or git!"

"You'd better listen to reason, Garth."

The old rawhider gripped his six-gun tighter, raising its muzzle. "And you'd better realize you're out of your bailiwick!"

Tulley shook his head. "Katie was right about you, Garth. You're not keeping up with the times. You give the orders on the G Bar L up to a point; then the law steps in. I represent the law, and I'm here on official business."

"Whose business? Webb Colter's business?"

Tulley stalled for time, hoping the old cowman

would start thinking and cool off. "Katie's business, Garth."

"What have you done now, Frank? Filed some kind of trumped-up charge against her?"

"You mean because of her trying to knock my brains out with the quirt? No. I forgave her for that. I want to talk to her about some stolen property."

"Are you speaking of the bronc the Simpson gal stole? It come here. I'll have the boys catch it up for you if you want it. Ain't worth twenty dollars."

"I'll tell Colter about it. I want to ask Katie about Colter's stolen land certificates."

Garth's brows lifted. "He lose them?"

"All of them."

"By God, I hope he don't find them," Garth exclaimed. He lowered the gun.

Tulley stepped into the hall. "Better bury the hatchet with Katie, Garth. You've been all wrong about her. Whatever she did, she did it for you and Effie."

Garth dropped his eyes. "She might have," he admitted. Features falling into lines of worry and defeat, he went through the routine of taking down the bracket lamp and blowing it out.

"Where do you want me to wait?" Tulley asked.

The rancher threw back his head then and called down the hall, "Effie, have you got a cup of coffee for Frank Tulley?"

A stove door banged back in the kitchen, but no reply came from there.

"Effie's still pouting," Garth said apologetically. "Wait in yonder, Frank. I'll have to roust Katie out of bed."

Lenzie had indicated the expensively cluttered-up parlour. Tulley entered the room and placed his hat on top of the organ. Wonderingly then, he contemplated a spindly, satin-bottomed chair that hadn't been here before Katie went East to that female-breaking corral. Gingerly, Tulley tested it. He found it amazingly strong. As big as he was, he couldn't even sway a creak out of it.

The distant rumble of Garth's voice sounded, and Tulley heard Effie say in high-pitched tones, "Well, let him go down to the cookshack. That's still G Bar L hospitality."

They continued to bicker.

It was fully ten minutes before Katie came into the parlour.

She'd belted a wrapper around her and had taken a few swipes at her ears with a hairbrush. Her eyes, usually big and brown, still contained sleep. She said, "Good morning, Frank," and stifled a yawn. Crossing to a heavy chair, she curled up on the arm of it.

"Why did you light out without me, Katie?"

"Didn't you want me to? All that trouble when you went to see about the buggy. Killing those men."

"Webb Colter killed Jules Carnotte. You were still at the hotel when I came to see him. Didn't you hear him call me sheriff?"

Katie nodded. "I heard you talking in the hall. I heard the racket in his room and watched you take him downstairs." Her mouth twisted with disdain. "He wasn't the man I thought he was."

Any other time Tulley would have been pleased by her criticism of his rival. Now her words had come too late to affect him.

He said, "Why didn't you wait till I got back, Katie?"

"I did wait. And you didn't come back."

"No," Tulley admitted, "I didn't. But I didn't want you to strike out alone. Why did you?"

"Well, because I knew Webb wouldn't stay in jail long, Frank, and I was afraid of him. He couldn't handle you, but he could me, and he would have taken his spite out on me."

"Somebody did turn him out."

"Calico Thompson? He and Webb are close friends."

"Calico says he didn't. I think Horace Aikens did it, hoping that Webb would be mad enough to jump me and I'd shoot him." He paused. "Someone stole Colter's scrip. Know anything about it?"

She smiled. "No. But let me tell you something, Frank. Those certificates are no good. They're counterfeit."

"Let me tell *you* something, Katie. Webb Colter

tore my room upside down looking for them. And he's been going around stepping on his underlip. If they are counterfeit, he sure is grieving over the loss of nothing."

Katie sat with a thoughtful expression in her eyes, the flush of a mounting indignation showing in her cheeks. "You think they're genuine?" she asked.

Tulley nodded.

Katie looked down at her ring. She twisted it on her finger. "Webb knew all along I couldn't love him, and he was very bitter about it. He was trying to get revenge on me, I suppose, telling me that. But he was really afraid of Daddy. Of our crew. He sure was scared of Obie Sheppard. Obie told him one time, 'If I ever hear of you mistreating Katie, I'm going to turn your gizzard wrongside out and peel it.' " She laughed. "Webb was always worrying that the G Bar L would start a war on the nesters."

"Well," Tulley said, "when a man wants a pretty girl and can't win her love, his love turns to hate, and that's the worst kind of hate there is."

"He really loved me," Katie murmured. "But I couldn't help it. He really meant well, too, when he explained about the Contreras Grant. He told me he was trying to force Daddy to keep up with the times, to get legal title to his land, like the other old-time cowmen were doing."

Webb had just been trying to learn how much

cold cash Garth could lay hands on, but Tulley didn't say as much to Katie. Her pride was injured enough, as it was.

"How's your head?" Katie asked presently.

"You nearly cracked my skull."

"Why, that couldn't be done, Frank Tulley," she scoffed. "I've seen you get thrown and land on your head and bounce like an india-rubber ball."

"I've got a soft head, Katie, and you have a hard heart."

"Fiddlesticks! How's your leg?"

"All right. I'm sound as a dollar, Katie. Except for being a mite lovesick."

"Well," she murmured, "I wish I could help you."

A sort of pleasant and comforting silence fell between them. Casting off the mood, Tulley reached into his pocket for Marie Simpson's deposition. He got up and handed it to Katie. "Read it."

Katie moved around to sit down in the armchair. As she perused the paper, Tulley watched her pretty face contort with outrage.

"That little hussy!" she blazed. "Why in the world would she tell such a lie, Frank?"

"Colter forced her to."

"And you've come to take Daddy back to jail, haven't you? If that girl swears to this in court—"

"She won't."

Katie handed the paper back, and Tulley said,

"Does Marie know your father by sight? I'm sure she would recognize him if she saw him riding by their place as usual. But would she know him close up, under different circumstances—if she saw him dressed like a teamster or preacher or something?"

"I don't know," Katie said. "I don't know that Daddy ever met her face to face."

"It's worth taking a chance on," Tulley said. He got his hat off the organ. "You understand that I'm taking Garth and Vince to town, trying to clear them, don't you, Katie? You won't interfere this time, will you?"

She stood before him, the top of her head coming even with his mouth. She looked dainty and fragile while at the same time there was an aura of lusty vigour about her.

"That star on your vest represents the law," she said. "We might block it a while, but we can't buck it for long. Do what you have to do, Frank. I'm going to my room and stay there. If you get yourself killed, it won't be my fault. If you do take Daddy to town, don't let anything happen to him."

"Don't worry. I killed one of the men guilty of the thing Garth is charged with, and Colter killed the other. When it comes to a showdown, I'll be on Garth's side, law or no law. But everything else aside, I got this badge by promising to bring Garth back and lock him up. I'm going to do it if I have to call in the army."

Throat uncommonly dry because he dreaded the chore at hand, Frank Tulley proceeded to the kitchen.

He found Garth and Effie seated at either end of the long table. Three places had been laid on the red-checked cloth, but Tulley knew that one was for Katie, not for him. He crossed to the china cupboard and helped himself to a cup and saucer. He made a trip to the stove and helped himself to coffee. He went over to stand by the door to the rear gallery then.

"If you've got a gun, Effie, you'll get your arm hurt again."

"You did hurt me, mister! My arm was black and blue." Above a tight, starched white collar, Effie's round face was mottled with anger.

"Katie almost split my head open with that quirt. That made us even, didn't it, Effie?" He took a sip of the scalding black coffee. "Garth," he said then, "I hear you lost your foreman."

"Yeah. And he was a good one, too. Outside of you, Frank, he had more cow savvy than anyone I know. A foreman like Gil Jebb is hard to come by."

"Who took his place?"

"Nobody yet. I'm going to have another talk with Gil and try to get him back. I'll give in to him, I reckon."

"What went wrong?"

"Me and him had a little difficulty about how to handle the nesters."

Tulley took a swallow of coffee. "Gil told me you had given the ramrod job to Obie Sheppard."

"No. Obie's too young."

Effie said, "Why, Garth, he's not either. You said when you were Obie's age—"

"I'm speaking of him, not myself."

Tulley said, "The younger, the better, Garth, for a fighting man."

"Ah, Frank, a man can't fight them cussed book laws and land statutes and suchlike."

"That's Katie's talk," Effie said. "You listen to that girl too much, Garth. I'm sorry now that we sent her off to school. It gave her biggety ideas."

Tulley emptied his cup and went back to the pot for more. "I pinned a deputy badge on Gil and sent him to Fort Griffin after a wanted man, Garth."

"So?"

"He may run for sheriff next election."

"How about you, Frank?"

"I won't run if Gil does," Tulley said. Noticing that the rancher hadn't touched his bacon and biscuits, he added, "Better fill up. We won't be packing no lunch."

Effie gave Tulley a direct look, a hard one. She said to her husband, "Don't go with him, Garth."

Tulley set his cup and saucer down and pulled Marie Simpson's statement from his pocket. He handed it to Effie.

She read it and said scornfully, "I'm not surprised. From what I've heard about Marie, I wouldn't put anything past her."

"What is it?" Garth asked.

Effie read it to him, with contempt and sarcasm.

Garth said, when she had finished, "I told you I didn't trust that Simpson gal. Getting rid of me will be a feather in her cap." He sighed. "Well, I had it coming to me for ever letting them clodhoppers get a toehold in this valley."

"Webb Colter's behind it," Effie sniffed.

"Of course. But he won't get away with it," Tulley said. He explained how he planned to trap Marie when she'd try to identify Garth as one of Burk's killers.

"That girl was right here in this house," Effie said. "She prowled around. Looked at our family album. May even be a picture of Garth in that room where you and Tom put her to bed. She'll put a rope around your neck, Garth, if you don't watch out."

"I'd better do what Frank says, Effie. He knows what's best for me." Having made a decision, the old rawhider fell to eating then, and emptied his coffee cup. "Get my hat, Effie."

"We'll go out the front way," Tulley said, when Garth got up from the table, "and take my horse."

Chapter Fourteen

Knowing that Garth and Effie would want a moment alone, Tulley went on along the hallway. He hoped to have another word with Katie. The girl had gone into her own room, however, and the door was closed. Spurs tinkling, Tulley continued on out to the front gallery.

The sun had climbed well above the eastern ridge now, spreading a hot glitter over everything except the patches of shade cast by the fences and trees and buildings. The cowhands had saddled up and ridden off, judging from the empty corrals, but one corral still had five saddle broncs in it, and one appeared to be Tulley's private mount. All in all, the ranch routine was going on as if Tulley's arrival had passed unnoticed. He knew it hadn't.

Hearing Garth dragging spurs along the hall, Tulley went down into the yard and unwrapped his bridle reins.

He led his horse and walked with Lenzie down the slope.

"I brought back those two horses that Ramage had in the county corral, Garth. They're down on the flat. You can get those saddles sometime when you're in town with the wagon."

"Uh-huh."

"We'll take it easy on the way back. I'll ride this same horse, and you can fork my dun gelding. If Vince didn't take to the timber when he saw me coming, he can ride that bronc of Colter's."

"Yeah," Garth muttered.

He checked his stride to glance back at the ranch house, his seamed face revealing worry.

"Sure going to be a scorcher," he said, walking on. He lifted his neckerchief and dabbed at his brow.

Tulley halted when they came even with the door of the cookshack. Handing Lenzie the bridle reins, he stepped back to get Tom Bradshaw's hat out of a saddlebag. He dusted it and shaped it and gave it a critical inspection. Satisfied, he took it into the building, and saw the flour-sack aproned figure of Bradshaw standing near the table where Jeffers and Potter and Sheppard sat.

Except for trickling cigarette smoke, the four of them might well have been wooden images.

Tulley held out the headpiece and said, "Much obliged for the use of your hat, Tom."

Bradshaw didn't move. He stared at Tulley and right through him. All at once then, the cook couldn't go through with it. "Ah, what the hell—you're plumb welcome, Frank," he said, and took the hat. "Been to beans yet?"

"No, but I tanked up on Effie's coffee," Tulley said.

He put his gaze on the waddy with the sorrel hair and freckled face.

"Well, Vince, what do you say we head for town? You and I and Garth have to play out the hands you and him drew while I was gone."

Potter reached for the cigarette dangling from his mouth. "What you really mean is, you want me and Garth to pay for your right to wear that star. You promised to put us back in jail if they would let you wear that tin badge, didn't you?"

"That was the bargain," Tulley admitted.

"Well," Potter said, "once was enough for me. I wouldn't go back to jail for Goddlemighty!"

"You'll go for Frank Tulley."

Cold, killing hostility showed in the features of the hawk-beaked Jeffers and the curly-haired Sheppard.

"Well, maybe you won't then, Vince," Tulley said. He turned away. The cook followed him over into the kitchen part of the room.

"Can your helper boil water yet, Tom?"

"He's coming right along. He'll make a better cookie than I am, one of these days."

"You're no cook, anyway. You're a sawbones, and a good one. Buffalo City sure needs you."

When Frank Tulley went outside, Garth was still standing there holding the horse, but his attention was fixed on his wife, coming down from the ranch house.

Within speaking distance, Effie called, "I've

changed my mind, Garth. I've got a feeling you're doing the wrong thing. You can't go."

Garth Lenzie bristled. "Who in hell are you trying to henpeck, Effie? Just keep your trap shut and go back where you belong."

"I'll not do it, mister!"

The hands were filing out of the cookshack now, Obie Sheppard in the lead.

Effie turned to him. "Obie, read the paper that Frank brought with him."

Sheppard swung his grey eyes on Tulley, who shifted the bridle reins and reached into his Levi's. He passed Marie's deposition to the curly-haired man. Sheppard read it with difficulty, forming some of the words with his lips.

He glanced up finally, eyes hot, and started to tear the paper into shreds.

"Don't!" Tulley said.

Sheppard's fingers froze. Reluctantly he handed the paper back. "Show me a *man* who'll tell a tale like that," he said bitterly, "and I'll kill him."

Tulley said, "I feel the same way, Obie."

Effie moved around to confront them both. "Obie," she said, "I don't want Garth or Vince to set foot off this ranch. If Frank took them to town, those grangers would start agitating for a hanging bee. I'm as much the boss of the G Bar L as Garth is, and I'm ordering you, Obie, and Cleon and Vince, to stand up to Frank Tulley."

Sheppard licked his lips. Jaws knotted, he

moved back a little. "You heard what she said, Sheriff. I reckon that's the way it'll have to be."

Tulley folded the paper and pushed it into a vest pocket, reins dangling from his right fingers.

"Don't lift your hackles at me, Obie. I'm not going to push it—try to prove I'm big enough to enforce the law single-handed. I came alone because I thought you fellows might be glad to have me on your side."

Sheppard was silent.

Jeffers said, "What do you mean by that, Frank?"

"Cleon," Tulley said, "I rode into Buffalo City with you and Obie for no other reason than to get Garth and Vince out of jail. I don't recall being particular about how we did it. I'll always favour the G Bar L. I can't help favouring it. But it will be in methods, not principles."

"You'll bring back a posse?" Effie asked.

"That seems to be the only answer, Effie. Whatever bloodshed there is will be on your head."

"Those are harsh words, Frank."

"They're true," Tulley said. He turned toward the corrals, leading the horse.

Bradshaw called, "Hold on, Frank."

Tulley stopped.

"I'm going with you," Bradshaw said.

"Quitting?" Garth asked.

"Yes. But you know it's not something I'm

doing on the spur of the moment, Garth. I've trained a man to take my place. I'm through ducking my responsibilities and being half a man. I'm going to town and do the work I was cut out to do. Doctoring."

The old rancher cleared his throat. "I wouldn't want to stop you, Tom. And I don't look on it as a parting of the ways."

"No, it's not that, Garth."

"You'll want to take your furniture and stuff. I expect I'd better have some of the hands hook a team to a wagon, eh?"

"I'll take a buckboard, Garth, and haul in only the things I'll need right away. Can't move it all till I get located."

Bradshaw rubbed a hand over his close-cropped head. "Frank," he said, "want to tie on behind and ride with me?"

"Good idea. I'll peel the saddle off of this horse and lead them both back. That is, if you'll have room for my saddle."

"Plenty of room," Bradshaw said. "While they're getting the rig ready, Frank, come in and let me fix you some breakfast."

As Tulley was eating, the three G Bar L hands came back in, ranging themselves before him, and the curly-haired man said, "If you bring a posse, you won't find us no different. We don't aim for Garth to be taken."

"We'll see, Obie."

Tulley put his attention on his plate then, ignoring their hostility, and presently they drifted back outside.

Two of the Mexican *braceros* brought a team and buckboard up behind the cookshack, and Tulley waited in the shade on the west side of the building, smoking a cigarette, while Bradshaw supervised loading of the rig.

Cleon and Obie and Vince had gone down to the corrals. Garth and Effie had returned to the ranch house. Tulley kept hoping that Katie would come down to say a parting word, but she didn't. She didn't even appear on the gallery.

Bradshaw was ready to pull out finally, and Tulley climbed up beside him.

Tooling the matched team of bays onto the road that curved down upon the short-grass flat, Bradshaw put a hand to his paunchy stomach. "Well, Frank, I won't have this potbelly much longer. The nesters will have me on the go twenty-four hours a day, or try to." He sighed. "But I'll enjoy it."

"That sounds like you've quit cussing yourself for letting that woman die."

"I have. The older a man gets, Frank, the more savvy he picks up. Suppose I did make a mistake and lose a life. It could be that I was just being used as a tool in a scheme I can't understand. My mistake wasn't intentional."

"You don't have to defend your actions to me,

Tom. What's that old saw about doctors burying their mistakes? They all make them."

Bradshaw was silent, lost in his own reflections.

Not being heavily loaded, the buckboard had a spring to it that took the jolts out of the road. Bradshaw made the bays step right along. They left the flat behind. With the sun quartering against their backs, they headed across the undulating mesquite land, the pale-coloured G Bar L longhorns grazing in all directions. Quite a way off to the left was the timber along the creek. Far ahead loomed Double Mountain. Bradshaw roused himself.

"What was that paper you showed Obie?"

"An eyewitness account of the Burk killing. Want to read it?"

"Later. Just tell me about it."

Tulley began with the gunshots that downed Al Ramage. He told of coming out of the county clerk's office and meeting Blake and Colter. He concluded with Marshal Aikens' doubting that Tulley could bring Garth and Vince to town without help.

Bradshaw thought it over. "Well, it was probably just the way Marie told it, Frank, except that Garth and Vince didn't enter into it at all. Carnotte and Spaugh were the two men all the way through."

"You're right, Tom," Tulley said, and repeated what Griff Spaugh had said that night in the county barn. He told of Carnotte's accusing Lige Wessels of killing Al Ramage. "You know Lige, Tom. Do you think he would have guts enough to meet Ramage face to face and shoot him?"

"All depends on how desperate he was."

With the harness slapping and jingling and the buckboard tyres grinding, the bays trotted down a slant and when they had topped out on the hog-back ridge of the far slope, Frank Tulley suddenly straightened on the seat. He pushed back his big white hat and pulled his sun-squinted eyes wide open.

Yonder against the wooded flanks of Double Mountain stood the charred ruins of Jess Burk's buildings, but they weren't deserted now. Someone had moved in there, because a covered wagon stood near Burk's well, and a team of mules, unharnessed, had been staked out to graze near the cross that marked Burk's grave.

Bradshaw said, "Looks like they're planning to stay."

"They won't," Tulley said.

When the rig drew near, three men emerged from the skeletal shadows of the barn.

"Pull up, Tom."

Stepping down to the ground, Tulley walked around behind the led horses and proceeded over to confront the nesters. One was a denim-clad fellow of middle age. The other two were younger and skinnier—the old man's sons, obviously. The youngest one clutched a double-barrelled shotgun.

"Howdy," Tulley said.

"Howdy-do, Sheriff." The old man spit out a stream of tobacco juice and sleeved his lips. "We was looking it over and estimating—"

"You lock that team of mules in the breeching and get back where you belong."

"Why, we ain't trespassing. This was Jess Burk's claim, and we aim to take it over. He was my wife's kin."

"Doesn't make a bit of difference. You fellows load up and get off of G Bar L range, or I'll see that you're buried right beside Jess yonder."

"Well, now, that's a funny way for an officer of the law to talk."

"Nothing funny about it," Tulley said. He glanced around. "Pull on down there in the shade and wait for me, Tom."

"Think it'll take long?" Bradshaw asked.

"We're not in any hurry. I figured we could spare them ten minutes."

The trespassing clodhopper and his two sons were already moving.

"Don't ever come past the mountain again."

"We won't. We'll leave as quick as we can get loaded up, Sheriff. But we've got a perfect right to be here. What chance has a law-abiding man got when the law's against him?"

"None."

Chapter Fifteen

It was nearly midnight when Frank Tulley came up from the county corrals to enter the courthouse by the back way. Just inside the door, he paused, listening. The noise was repeated—a snortlike snore. Made by a prisoner in that last cell.

Well, it could be someone that Marshal Aikens had jailed, and Tulley saw no need of waking him up just to find out who he was.

Continuing along the corridor, footsteps resounding loud in the deserted building, Tulley got out the key and let himself into his office, slamming the door behind him with considerable force.

"Calico?"

No reply came from the room containing the bunks.

Going on back, Tulley struck a lucifer. He was alone. Having been on his way to his hotel room, he now changed his mind. He would sleep here. He took off his clothes and lay down on one of the cots. It was a long while before he could force thoughts of Katie Lenzie and G Bar L affairs from his mind, but finally he did, and slept.

Arising early, he went down to the corrals and saddled his dun gelding and rode up Yeguas

Creek, spent half an hour immersed to his chin in the summer-warm water, and rode back. Tying up behind the courthouse, he saw Calico Thompson coming down the sidewalk, carrying a familiar box used as a tray for toting grub and coffee from the hotel kitchen to the jail. Calico had nothing to do with feeding Marshal Aikens' prisoners, so it could mean only one thing: Gil Jebb had returned from Fort Griffin.

Tulley went on in and looked through the bars at the prisoner, who sat on the steel frame of the bunk.

"You look sort of peaked, Lige."

The prisoner said, "Howdy, Frank."

"Any gunplay between you and my deputy?"

"No. I was sitting in a poker game and he sneaked up behind me and rammed the muzzle of his gun against my head. Shaking like a leaf, by God. I let him call the turns from then on."

"Know why you're locked up?"

"He said it was for killing Al Ramage."

"Did you?"

"I ain't going to own up to anything. How about some chuck?"

"Calico's coming with it."

Tulley stepped back, and presently, with his battered hat pulled low on one bushy-browed eye, Calico Thompson shuffled in, carrying the tray. He looked at Tulley. "Well, son, Deputy Jebb got his man, but it appears like you didn't."

Tulley made no reply.

Setting the box down, Calico knelt to slide a plate of stew and a mug of coffee under the steel lattice of the door. "If this ain't enough grub, Lige, just holler. A condemned man is entitled to a bellyful."

"How about a drink of whisky, then?"

"Eat, first," Calico said. "And when the sheriff leaves, I'll see what I can do about it."

Picking up his food, Wessels turned back to sit on the bunk.

Tulley said, "I don't care if he has a drink. Go get him one, Calico."

Wessels grinned. "You don't hate killers as much as Deputy Jebb does, eh, Frank?"

"Why should I? I'm one, myself. You heard what happened to your saddlemates, didn't you?"

"Yeah."

"Colter shot Jules," Tulley said. "In the back. Any idea why?"

"Griff and Jules double-crossed Webb."

"They weren't supposed to kill Jess Burk?"

"No. Jess was in on it, himself. He was going to co-operate with them and make it look bad for the G Bar L. They were supposed to burn him out and make it look like they had beat him up—make it look like the G Bar L had done it."

Tulley understood now what the dying Griff Spaugh had wanted to say: "—but Webb Colter didn't tell us to kill Jess." To the man in the cell, Tulley said, "You make things look better for Colter, Lige."

"Can't help it. It's the truth."

After a moment, Tulley said, "Whoever killed Al Ramage will probably hang for it."

"I'll bet you the best saddle horse in the valley against your six-shooter that he doesn't."

Tulley stared at him. "Did you shoot at Marie Simpson?"

"I fired my gun."

Tulley said, "I've got a feeling I've been all wrong about you, Lige." He turned away.

He went to his office, expecting to find his deputy there, but Jebb hadn't showed up. He was taking it easy, doubtless, after his long vigil with Wessels. Jebb probably hadn't dared to nap. Still seeing no clear-cut course of action for himself, Tulley went upstairs to return Marie's statement to Fred Blake, but the attorney wasn't at his desk.

Webb Colter was in Tulley's office when Tulley came back downstairs.

Colter stood at a window near the keg of bourbon, and he swung around. He was freshly barbered and spruced up, and his dark eyes smouldered with repressed excitement. Tulley sensed a recklessness in him, and ascribed it to Wessels having been brought back and jailed.

"Ready to have that drink with me, Sheriff?"

"I am, if you feel like you need to copper a bet for today."

Crossing to his desk, Tulley rolled the top down. "Webb," he said, "Katie Lenzie didn't take your land certificates."

"Why, hell, I told you she didn't get them."

"Then who did?"

"You let me worry about that. What's the reason you didn't bring Garth in?"

Tulley said, "You let me worry about that." He joined Colter at the keg.

Colter drew. "Say when," he said.

"Three fingers."

"A man's drink."

"Then you had better draw one that size for yourself, Webb."

They raised the tin cups.

"To Katie's wedding," Colter said.

"Not this one. Let's drink to Lige Wessels."

Colter showed his white teeth. "To Lige's neck."

They tossed off the bourbon, and Tulley said, "You sure have got the jitters, Webb."

"Sure. Everyone has. We're all wondering when you're going over and get Garth Lenzie and lock him up."

Tulley stared.

Colter said, "He's over at the hotel. They followed you and Bradshaw to town. Garth and Effie and Katie."

"And Sheppard and Potter and Jeffers, huh?"

Colter nodded.

"Hunting trouble," Tulley said.

He tossed his cup down with a clatter and went over to his swivel chair. He sank down in it, gaunt face immobile.

"Is Gil Jebb over at the hotel?" he asked presently.

"He's in his room. He came down and ate breakfast and went back to bed. Don't look to him for help. Or to anyone else. Folks are betting on it now."

"On what?"

"Some are betting that you'll put Garth back in jail. Others say you'll tuck your tail and run."

"How are you betting, Webb?"

Colter reset his hat. "I can't make up my mind how bad you want Katie."

"I don't want her bad enough to lose my self-respect," Tulley said, and then he added, "I don't have any choice."

"What do you mean?"

"I gave Horace Aikens my word, and he's expecting me to keep it. It's no longer a question of Garth's being guilty or not guilty—I know he isn't. But he's a pawn between me and the marshal now, and if I break my word to Aikens, I couldn't beat him to the draw. He would have the edge on me."

Colter shrugged. "I don't understand you."

"You're no gunman."

"No. I'm not what you would call a gunman. But I carry a gun."

Tulley gave him a hard smile. "And you're afraid to use it," he said derisively. Sobering then, Frank Tulley said, "I'm afraid to use mine, too, Webb, right now."

He took his gunbelt off.

Chapter Sixteen

Leaving Colter in the office, Tulley went outside to pause for a moment on the courthouse steps. He looked toward the hotel and saw that the three G Bar L hands had planted themselves in chairs on the veranda, obviously to keep watch on the lobby door. They knew that Tulley wouldn't dare use the rear entrance. If he did, he would be laughed out of town.

Rigs and delivery hacks rattled along the streets, along a background of saloon music, the dust of their passing floating in the hot sunshine. Tulley was conscious of the clangour of hammered metal and of the countless small noises of home and corral and chicken yard. Over in front of Pemberton's store a sodbuster coughed with exaggerated violence and spat. The hitching rails were crowded, and there were more than the usual number of loungers under the awnings of the business places.

Tulley noticed Fred Blake then.

The attorney was hurrying across from Marshal Aikens' office. Lifting a hand in greeting, Tulley went down the courthouse steps.

"Hold on, Frank."

"Not now, Fred. I'll see you after a bit."

"Wait, Frank—the girl's gone! Marie ran off from my wife and she took a Colt .44 with her."

Tulley waited for the attorney to come up. "She probably went home, Fred. She'll be all right."

The attorney's face was strained. "But I'm afraid they'll kill her. Do you still have her statement?"

"Yes, here in my pocket. I've got some other business to attend to right now, Fred, and then we'll see about Marie. All right?"

Reluctantly the attorney nodded, and Tulley went on across the plaza.

By the time he had reached the hotel veranda, he'd decided that he would try his hand with Vince Potter first.

Tulley didn't ascend the steps. He walked up to the edge of the veranda in front of the sorrel-haired man.

"You're under arrest, Vince. Hand over your gun, and let's go."

Potter's freckled face twisted in a sneer. He glanced at Obie Sheppard. The curly-haired man had his chair tilted against the wall, hat pulled down even with his eyebrows.

Jeffers was seated on Potter's right.

They all wore six-shooters. Deliberately staring at the place Tulley's gunbelt should have been, Potter said contemptuously, "You go to hell."

Tulley looked at Cleon Jeffers, a friend of long standing. "Cleon," he said, "you and I have been saddlemates, but I've got a star on now. I'm going to have to teach this smart aleck here some respect for it. Are you joining him, or keeping out of it?"

"I ride for the brand," Jeffers said, "and we all figure it's a damned sight bigger than that badge you're packing."

Frank Tulley moved fast. Planting his hands on the veranda floor, he leaped upon it and was crouched there by the time Potter was out of the chair. He punched Potter in the stomach. Potter yelled and doubled forward. Tulley slewed sidewise to meet Obie Sheppard. Evading Sheppard's clawing hands, Tulley slugged him on the temple. Sheppard was rocked backwards. Flailing the air wildly, he fell off the veranda.

Jeffers rammed into Tulley and sought a grip on his throat that would choke him. Jeffers was whining like an animal. Tulley jack-knifed forward. Jeffers hurtled over him. Stumbling over a chair, Jeffers kicked it aside and whirled, reaching for his gun, face viciously contorted. Tulley ran forward. He felled Jeffers with a blow to the chin, but Jeffers held on to his six-shooter. Tulley drove a boot into his ribs and managed to stomp the weapon out of the man's hands. Jeffers was crying real tears when Tulley staggered about aimlessly, stunned by a blow from Vince Potter.

Stumbling over the chair that had tripped Jeffers, Tulley rammed his head against the wall, and it seemed to clear his mind. He grappled with Potter, and drove his shoulder into Potter's underjaw. Potter went backward with a gurgling gasp.

Sheppard was upon Tulley again, pounding him with both fists. They battered each other, grunting with the force of the blows. They went down clawing, rolling over and over, and tumbled off the veranda, with Tulley nearly losing a boot when his spur caught on the edge.

He saw the muzzle of Sheppard's six-gun coming around, and jerked his head an instant before the weapon roared, half-deafening him. He put all his strength into a struggle for the gun and got it. He struck at Sheppard's curly head and saw the blond hair darken with blood.

All at once Tulley became conscious of his surroundings, of the twisted faces of the crowd, of the roars. He looked up into Katie Lenzie's face. Katie was screeching at him, "Stop hitting him, Frank Tulley, or I'll kill you!"

"He's all yours, Katie," Tulley mumbled.

He pushed away from Sheppard, got to his feet and stumbled back a few steps.

Throwing herself upon the curly-haired man Katie sobbed, "Oh, Obie, Obie—!"

Frank Tulley stood there looking straight at Tom Bradshaw without recognizing him.

"Are you all right, Frank?"

Tulley nodded.

He saw that Vince Potter was still on the veranda, hunkered over now, spitting out specks of blood.

"Let's go, Vince."

Potter nodded.

Reeling, staggering like a drunken man, Potter permitted himself to be escorted through the crowd and on to the plaza and back to a cell.

"Well! Well!" Lige Wessels chortled. "I've seen everything now!"

Tulley got Potter locked up, and stood there a moment, nauseated. He made it into the corridor and into his office. He reached his swivel chair and sat there shaking his head, as though he had water in his ear.

When his mind had cleared, he got up and went to the bourbon keg and drew a cup brimming full. He spilled some, but got enough down his throat to revive him as it burned through his veins.

Except for tattered clothing, cuts and bruises, blood and sweat and dust, he was all right, he assured himself. And he had jailed Vince Potter.

Garth would be next.

It wasn't thoughts of Garth Lenzie himself that made Tulley sigh. It was something deeper. Tulley had followed a dream back to this valley and had watched that dream crumble. He had built an image of the woman he wanted, he supposed, and had forced Katie Lenzie to fit the pattern.

Well, Doc Bradshaw had made a mistake and had pulled out of it. Frank Tulley could, too.

Calico Thompson's shuffle sounded in the corridor, but the oldster came only to the doorway. He elaborately ignored Tulley's battered appearance.

Tulley said, "Where did Colter go?"

"Over to the Cowman's Ruin. Want me to go get him?"

"No." Tulley lowered his gaze, inspecting himself again. "Might go up to my room and get me some clothes, though."

"What kind do you want?"

"Like these."

Calico had scarcely gone when the tread of many boots sounded, coming toward the courthouse steps. Tulley took a stand beside his desk, waiting.

Deputy Jebb and Garth Lenzie entered the office first. Bankston and Pemberton and Mullins came in with them. County Attorney Fred Blake appeared in the doorway, but he moved off again when the corridor began filling with sodbusters.

Lenzie was bareheaded. His shirt sleeves were rolled up, his vest unbuttoned, and his pockets stuffed with cigars. He wore no gun.

"Lock me up, too, Frank," he said.

Tulley ignored him for the moment. Swinging his gaze on the deputy, Tulley said, "I don't need your help any longer, Gil. Did I tell you to bring Garth in?"

"I didn't," Jebb said. He took off his badge and laid it on the desk. "Garth told me if I wanted the foreman job back, I could have it, and I took it."

Tulley looked from one to the other. "All settled between you, huh?"

Jebb said, "Only trouble I ever had was with Tom Bradshaw. He got to where he thought he owned the G Bar L. With him not there, Garth and me will get along fine."

"Go ahead and cuss Tom," Tulley said. "He's not here."

Jebb's eyes hardened. Whirling about, he stalked from the office, the double-chinned Ben Mullins swinging a stare at his back.

"Well," Mullins wheezed, "we can't count on Gil Jebb running for sheriff."

Tulley said, "You can count on me, Ben. I like this job."

"Black eye and all, eh?"

"I'll be more careful next time, Ben."

Out in the corridor one of the sodbusters said, "Tulley, ain't no use of you running for sheriff if you don't come up with the man who killed Al Ramage."

"Gil Jebb brought him in, didn't he?"

"No, sir, he didn't."

Tulley said, "They tell me that Lige was

courting one of your women. Is that why you're defending him?" No one answered, and Tulley said, "I don't believe Wessels killed Ramage, either, but it's not for me to say."

"I'll vote for you, Tulley," a whiskered granger said. "By thunder, you don't play no favourites. No danger of you joining a courthouse crowd to rob us."

"It'll take votes to elect me, men. You've all got one apiece, and I'd like to have them."

John Pemberton said, "I think you'll get them, Frank."

He and Bankston and Mullins left the office together. Tulley shut the door behind them, and the gathering in the corridor dispersed.

Tulley then said to Garth Lenzie, "Marie Simpson's statement has got me worried. She'd never have said what she did if she hadn't been scared to death of Webb Colter. I don't think Webb would harm her, but I may be wrong. I think you'll be safe in my jail, but I could be wrong about that. Want a six-shooter to keep with you?"

"Not unless you'll give Vince one."

"The hell with him," Tulley said. "He can take his chances."

"With what?"

"Justice."

Strain showing in his face, Lenzie said, "Frank, I come here because the Simpson gal told me to. She's on my side now. Nobody'll get her to testify against me, not even Webb Colter. Fact is, she'll testify for me. She seen Jules Carnotte and Griff Spaugh kill Jess Burk."

"I know that, Garth, but what if she's found dead somewhere on G Bar L range? This statement might be enough then to put a rope around your neck. I can't tear it up. The county attorney expects me to give it back to him. And he didn't see and hear what Marie saw and heard, and he wasn't with me when I shot Spaugh." Tulley drew a deep breath. "Hell, I don't know. You just talked with Marie? Where did you see her?"

"Never mind."

Garth's tone and expression imparted the idea that Marie was at the hotel, in the Lenzie quarters, probably.

"It's time for me to lock you up, Garth. I don't know how long you'll stay there. That's up to Fred Blake. As far as I'm concerned, I'll be ready to turn you out when Horacc Aikens sees you."

"You'll do that?"

"No. I'd have to resign if I did, and I want to hang on to this badge."

"Well, between you and that Simpson gal, Frank, I'm feeling a damned sight easier than I did. Hope you don't hold no grudge against Effie."

"You let Effie worry about that, Garth. That's our business."

Tulley motioned for the rancher to precede him into the corridor.

Calico Thompson was there with new clothes when Tulley returned to the office. Tulley changed into them and hurled his tattered garments into the wastebasket.

He said, “Stick around close, Calico. I’m going to take another swig of that bourbon and pile down in yonder for some rest.”

“I’ll set here at your desk, son, and tell everybody to keep out.”

Tulley said dryly, “Everyone but Marshal Aikens, that is.”

Calico shrugged.

Nightfall was settling over the town when Tulley awakened. Sore and stiff, he seemed to ache in every joint and muscle. What really made him wince at each breath was a cracked rib cage. A G Bar L hand had kicked him. But he had to keep going anyway.

Looking to his six-gun, he got his hat, and found Calico Thompson seated at the desk.

“Been there all afternoon?”

“Most of the time.”

“Fed the prisoners?”

“Not yet.”

“Anyone give you any trouble?”

“That there county attorney has. He’s run up and down the stairs all evening seeing if you was awake.”

"I know what's the matter with him," Tulley said, "but I can't help him any."

Calico left soon, to bring Garth and Vince and Lige the evening meal.

Tulley sat alone in the darkened office, arousing when Thompson came in and lit the lamps.

"I feel like hell, Calico. I'm going over to the hotel and go to bed. You stay awake and guard those prisoners."

Stepping back to the desk, Tulley picked up the badge Gil Jebb had laid there.

"Turn around here, Calico. I'm going to swear you in as my deputy."

"Me?" The oldster's features worked emotionally.

"Sure. I told you that you could keep your job until something better turned up. This is it."

Frank Tulley was conscious of the curious stares of the other guests as he went through the lobby, and one man, a drummer, stepped in front of him to appraise the damage inflicted upon his physiognomy by G Bar L fists. It was all part of the job, Tulley figured. Raising a friendly hand at the clerk, he made it to the stairway, and finally to the second floor. When he reached his bed, he fell across it with his clothes on, and promptly went to sleep.

Chapter Seventeen

Something, perhaps an outcry, awakened Frank Tulley. Instantly alert, he rolled over and swung his boots off the bed, and then, somewhere on this upper floor, a six-gun exploded.

Tulley stood up and limped across the room, and at this moment someone ran down the hall.

Stepping into the dimly lighted hallway himself, Tulley saw a small denim-clad figure headed for the outside stairway. It was Marie Simpson.

She had come out of Webb Colter's room, leaving the door ajar. Tulley went that way, and found Colter slumped in one of the red plush chairs. He was badly hurt, groaning and clutching his chest. His fingers were red.

He had been sitting there in shirt sleeves and moccasins, talking with Marie, apparently, and she had shot him. A Colt .44 lay on the rug, still smoking.

Someone else was rushing up the stairs now. It was Walter. Hurrying in, he stopped suddenly to stand transfixed. He licked his lips.

"What happened?"

Tulley said, "What did happen, Webb?"

"Acci-accident. Trying the action on that gun and shot myself."

So Colter knew that the gun was lying there

on the rug. He must have seen Marie drop it. Or they might have been scuffling for possession of the weapon.

Walter said, “Doctor in town now, Mr. Colter. I know where he’s playing poker.” Without waiting for a reply, Walter whirled around and trotted from the room.

“Want some liquor, Webb?”

Colter found grim amusement in that. “Listen, Sheriff. Horace Aikens stole my land certificates. Get them from him. Give them to Garth Lenzie.”

“What about your other property?”

“People in Missouri. My will—”

“Hang on, Webb.”

“Get the land—give them—tell him I’m sor—”

“I’ll do it, Webb. I really will.”

Webb Colter was in a coma when the clerk returned with Doctor Bradshaw and several others, Ben Mullins and John Pemberton with them. Hotel guests gathered in the hall behind them, but Katie and Effie Lenzie weren’t there.

Bradshaw took a look at the man slumped in the chair. He glanced at the gun. “Who shot him?”

Walter said, “It was an accident.” He repeated what Colter had said. Tulley corroborated it.

Bradshaw grunted.

John Pemberton said, “If that’s the way Webb wanted it, that’s the way it’ll have to be, Tom.”

Frank Tulley made no mention of having seen Marie Simpson race down the hall. Some of the other guests might have seen her, too, but it wouldn't matter, in view of Colter's explanation.

Bradshaw felt Colter's pulse and frowned. He lifted an eyelid, then said in a disappointed monotone, "I didn't have a chance to save him."

Frank Tulley was down on the street twenty minutes later, hunting Horace Aikens. The marshal's office was lighted, but Aikens wasn't there. Searching among the crowd in the Cowman's Ruin Saloon, Tulley then came back toward the hotel but turned the corner toward Mexican-town.

Along this street, amid odours of cooking food and cactus whisky and stable ammonia, music of a string band emanated from Francisca's Place. Immediately upon entering, Tulley saw Aikens, but not before the marshal had observed him. Flat black hat cocked on the back of his long, narrow head, Aikens was seated with two well-dressed *ganaderos* from over on the Brazos.

Several stacks of gold coin gleamed on the green baize.

Lifting a hand in greeting, Aikens then resumed his conversation with the *ganaderos.*

The spacious adobe wasn't so crowded at this hour, but customers ranged along the bar. They weren't drinking. They had their backs to the mahogany while watching one of the *señoritas* tap her high heels as she wriggled about the dance floor. She finished with a graceful twist that spun her red skirt high. As applause made a din of the place, Tulley walked toward Aikens' table.

Something in Tulley's face brought the tall, stooped marshal out of his chair. He grasped the edge of his coat.

Becoming alarmed, one of the fat *ganaderos* cried, "*Señor*, permit me to complete this transaction and depart in peace."

Tulley made no reply. He kept his gaze on Aikens. "Webb Colter was killed a while ago. Did you know that?"

"Yes. And I was sorry to hear it. Accident, eh?"

"That's what he said. And that puts me on his side. He also said you stole his land certificates."

Aikens' thick-lidded eyes brightened. "He was just trying to cause trouble."

"Isn't that what you've been wanting?"

The fat Mexican became even more frightened as Francisca's Place began to lose customers. Eyes round, he sawed in his chair, casting a glance at the floor, and Tulley realized that Colter's carpetbag was on the other side of the table, between the two chairs.

Tulley said, "You're under arrest, Aikens, for killing Al Ramage. Bring that carpetbag and come on."

For several seconds Tulley was in doubt about Aikens' intentions. Aikens wasn't coming. Tulley's hand slapped down to his Remington. The concussion of it and the gun Aikens snatched from his shoulder holster was deafening. The lamps guttered, eerie light flickering over the clouding gunsmoke. Shot in the brow as his own gun drilled a hole in the ceiling, Aikens fell dead, sending his chair careening backward.

Tulley moved closer. "Hand me that carpet-bag."

Hastily the fat *ganadero* swung the bag on to the table.

Tulley took it and strode out.

He walked back to the corner and met Calico Thompson coming from the hotel.

"What did they do with Webb?"

"Left him in his room for tonight. I should have set up with him, but Walter put me out and locked the door."

They walked on to the plaza and went around to the back, Tulley explaining about Aikens.

Opening the cells to free Garth and Vince, Tulley handed the rancher the carpetbag. "It's Colter's land certificates. He said give them to you, and that he was sorry. You can get title to all your range now."

Lenzie and Potter hurriedly left.

Ignoring Wessels' demand that he be informed of his fate now that the real killer of Al Ramage was dead, Tulley and Calico headed for the office. They had scarcely reached it when Fred Blake rushed in.

"Colter and Aikens both dead?" he asked.

"Uh-huh," Tulley said. He recounted what had occurred.

The attorney seemed badly shaken. "I told my wife she ought to have kept closer watch on Marie. Frank, you ought to let Wessels go. Horace did kill Al. Al and I left here together that night, and met Horace. He said his plans were all made and he wasn't going to change them on my account. He whipped out his gun and emptied it into Al without saying a word to Al. Then Horace sent Wessels on a trumped-up errand out of town to lay a false trail, and I doubt that Wessels knew why. He and I were in the same boat—scared to death of Horace."

"I wasn't what you would call contemptuous of him, myself, Fred. Calico, go back there and turn Lige Wessels loose."

"What'll I tell him, son?"

"Say, 'Lige, you get out of the valley and don't come back.' He won't ask you any questions."

Tulley wrote to Mose and Maudie Simpson, telling them to come home, then he turned in.

He left Buffalo City, himself, before daylight. He took the Double Mountain road, trailing Marie, hoping to find her at home.

At the Simpson place, Blake's hired hand told him that Marie had been there. She had stayed all night and had packed her saddle for a long trip, saying she was headed for New Mexico.

The hired hand wondered why, but Tulley

didn't tell him. After a big meal, he saddled a fresh horse and rode on. At the flat below the G Bar L headquarters he cut a change of mounts out of the remuda, and headed south-west, straight for the headwaters of Yeguas Creek. Where the trail lifted out of the valley, he searched carefully for signs.

There were none left by Marie.

Perhaps Tulley had ridden around her. The disheartening part of it was, he might not have. She might not have told the truth about her destination.

Reining the G Bar L horse about, Tulley rode back down into the valley. He crossed the creek. He pulled up among the trees at the spot where the remnants of his burned trail outfit were scattered about the charcoal smudges of his old campfire.

He sat his saddle, staring morosely at nothing.

Suddenly, off there in the brush, he heard a stick pop. Lifting his head, he peered in that direcion. He saw nothing, but some inner something informed him that Marie was sitting her horse there in that thicket.

Tulley dismounted. He ground-tied his horse and picked up a limb to break into firewood. Looking toward the thicket he asked, "What are you running for, Marie? Webb Colter said that he shot himself accidentally. He didn't even mention your name."

"But you saw me. You know what I did."

"Sometimes you have to do things like that. You shot him so he wouldn't force you to commit the perjury that would get Garth Lenzie hung."

"Webb died?"

"Yeah."

"Well—" Her voice broke off as though tear-choked. There was a stir in the thicket, and Marie rode out of it on a sorrel mare. She was wearing Levi's, and swung gracefully down from her saddle, which was packed with bedroll and saddlebags.

Tulley said, "Here's my old can. Have you got any coffee?"

"Yes." Her eyes were filled with tears.

Tulley got a fire going and went to the creek for water.

"Fred Blake tore up that paper we signed and wiped the slate clean all the way around. Aikens had stolen Colter's land certificates, as you probably know. Webb told me to get them and give them to Garth Lenzie. I had to kill Aikens."

She got coffee and grub from her pack and silently began preparing a meal.

Tulley said, "I'm going to run for sheriff next election, and everyone says I'll win. A law officer's job is always dangerous. He's not safe even in his own home. But if he's got a wife with sand enough to back him up, ain't much he has to worry about. I sure would hate to have a woman who bellyached when I had to use the tools of my trade."

"Guns?"

Tulley nodded.

She took a deep breath, and when she expelled it, she smiled at him. He smiled back.

Center Point Large Print
600 Brooks Road / PO Box 1
Thorndike, ME 04986-0001 USA

(207) 568-3717

US & Canada:
1 800 929-9108
www.centerpointlargeprint.com